"I can't think of another woman who shares your unique skill set.

"You see, I need someone who understands that our 'relationship' is just for show. Someone who can play a part under pressure. Persuade people that she's something she's not. Lie to their faces." His eyes locked with hers. "Someone willing and available to bend to my will."

Her pupils flared. "Then you definitely need to choose another woman, because I'm neither of those things."

Watching her face, Tiger wondered what it was exactly about this woman that drew him to her so intensely. It was maddening to feel this way, but to not understand why...

Most likely it was just this whole setup, he reassured himself. He was intrigued, or maybe that wasn't the right way to describe how he was feeling, but he couldn't think of a better one.

"You misunderstand me, Sydney." He saw her hands ball into fists as he used her name. "When I said *willing and available*, I meant within the context of the alternative being jail time."

Ruthless Rivals

Let the billion-dollar battle commence...

The feud between billionaire CEOs Tiger McIntyre and Harris Carver is legendary. Once, the determined and outrageously handsome duo were a force to be reckoned with. Until a perceived betrayal put an abrupt end to their friendship and ignited a ferocious rivalry... They just never expected it to put them in the paths of the only women with the power to take them—and their *hearts*—down for good!

When Tiger discovers his new assistant is actually a hacker working for the enemy, he uses the unfortunate situation to his advantage. By demanding that Sydney's next act is being his fake date in Venice!

Boss's Plus-One Demand
Available now!

After his attempt to bring down his rival backfired spectacularly, Harris needs to do some damage control. Only, his new PR manager is the woman he spent one passion-filled night with! And she's carrying a scandalous surprise...

Don't miss Harris and Eden's story, coming soon!

BOSS'S PLUS-ONE DEMAND

LOUISE FULLER

Harlequin

PRESENTS

**Harlequin®
PRESENTS™**

ISBN-13: 978-1-335-93945-6

Boss's Plus-One Demand

Copyright © 2024 by Louise Fuller

Harlequin Enterprises ULC
22 Adelaide St. West, 41st Floor
Toronto, Ontario M5H 4E3, Canada
www.Harlequin.com

Printed in Lithuania

MIX
Paper | Supporting
responsible forestry
FSC® C021394

Louise Fuller was a tomboy who hated pink and always wanted to be the prince—not the princess! Now she enjoys creating heroines who aren't pretty pushovers but are strong, believable women. Before writing for Harlequin, she studied literature and philosophy at university, then worked as a reporter on her local newspaper. She lives in Royal Tunbridge Wells with her impossibly handsome husband, Patrick, and their six children.

Books by Louise Fuller

Harlequin Presents

The Italian's Runaway Cinderella
Maid for the Greek's Ring
Their Dubai Marriage Makeover
Returning for His Ruthless Revenge
Her Diamond Deal with the CEO

Hot Winter Escapes

One Forbidden Night in Paradise

Behind the Billionaire's Doors...

Undone in the Billionaire's Castle

The Diamond Club

Reclaimed with a Ring

Visit the Author Profile page
at Harlequin.com for more titles.

CHAPTER ONE

Harris Carver's private members' club, New York

'IF YOU'D LIKE to follow me, Ms Truitt. Mr Carver is waiting for you in the members' lounge.'

The man in the suit turned and Sydney Truitt followed him. She had no idea where she was. She had been picked up at the airport and then driven by limousine into an underground car park. But this must be some kind of private club, she thought as she followed the man in the suit along the wood-panelled corridor.

He stopped in front of a door, knocked briskly and then opened it and took a step back to allow her to pass. 'Mr Carver will see you now.'

At first she thought the room was empty, but then she saw him.

As Harris Carver rose to his feet and walked towards her, she felt her shoulders tense. Up until now, most of her clients had been smaller businesses, but there weren't many businesses as big as HCI.

'Ms Truitt.' He held out his hand and she shook it. 'Thank you for meeting me here, and for signing the NDA. I know it must all feel a little "cloak and dagger" but, given my position, it's best, I find, to err on the side of caution.'

She smiled politely. 'Of course. And thank you for considering me for the contract, although I'm not actually sure what it is I'm being considered for.' The phone call had been brief and vague enough that she had been slightly afraid that they had called the wrong person.

'It's a short-term contract. Just three days but you will be handsomely rewarded for your time. Take a seat.'

'Could I just ask why you've approached me? It's just there are bigger and better-known people who do what I do—' She could think of at least two firms of white hat hackers here in New York who could carry out a legitimate 'attack' on HCI to find and fix any possible security issues within its network, and yet he had chosen her.

He shrugged. 'I had a shortlist of suitable candidates. Everyone was on a par skill-wise but it was your background that gave you the edge.' He hesitated and then he smiled, a predatory smile that made her whole body grow still and tense. 'You see, I need someone who is not just technically capable but who is, how can I put it?' He paused. 'Ah, yes, ethically flexible. Growing up in your family would suggest you have that quality.'

'My family?' She frowned. This wasn't how these conversations normally went. 'What do you know about my family?'

He held her gaze. 'This contract is sensitive. I needed to know that you would be fit for purpose, so I had my people take a closer look. Don't worry. They're thorough but discreet.' Still holding her gaze, he paused, his face expressionless. 'Unlike your brothers, who seem to have made quite a name for themselves with the local law enforcement in your home town.'

He was right. All three of her brothers had followed the same well-trodden path as their father and uncles. Only, that was the problem. They had the wrong role models and even before they could walk or talk, people had made assumptions about them. But they didn't know them as she did. Just because they had criminal records didn't mean they were bad to the bone, because they weren't. Far from it.

'My brothers are not—' she began, but he held up his hands placatingly.

'I'm not judging, just stating the facts, which are that they have broken the law and are now facing the consequences. I'm sure you must be anxious to help them, but help is so expensive, I find. The good kind anyway. The kind that delivers the required result. Which is why I think you're the perfect fit for this job.' He paused again, his grey gaze sweeping over her assessingly. 'I think you are someone who can help me.'

She swallowed. 'Help you do what?'

'It's a business matter. Tiger McIntyre has stolen something from me. A piece of intellectual property. I want it back. I need it back so that I can prove he did what he will undoubtedly deny doing. Which means I need someone on the inside. Someone who can pose as an employee while she hacks into his server.'

Harris Carver's voice faded and thinned, swallowed up by the heavy, persistent thud of her heartbeat. He wanted her to pose as an employee? Was he out of his mind? Tiger McIntyre had a reputation for being as fearsome and ruthless as his namesake. And as beautiful. Her pulse accelerated. Not that she had met him, but she had seen his picture often enough that she could almost picture his sculpted face and arresting gaze.

'It will mean crossing a line so I understand if that's giving you pause for thought.'

Harris Carver was leaning forward slightly and she blinked, trying to refocus her mind.

'You're a very wealthy, powerful man, Mr Carver, so I wanted to give you the chance to pretend that I misunderstood what you were suggesting. Because it's not just crossing a line, it's illegal.'

He held her gaze for a few uncomfortable seconds and she had to clench her jaw to stop herself from looking away.

'Something which your family knows all about.'

She got to her feet unsteadily. This was not who she was. It was not even who her brothers were, deep down. Only explaining that would mean revealing more than she was willing to do, had ever done, because even just thinking about it still had the power to make her shake inside.

'But I'm not my family so I'm afraid I'm going to have to decline your offer because if I get caught it would ruin my reputation—'

'Then don't get caught.' She felt her muscles tense as Harris Carver typed something onto his phone and then held it out so that she could see the numbers flashing on the screen.

'Just so you know how appreciative I would be.'

Her eyes widened. That was a lot of money.

'Very appreciative,' he said then, and he touched the screen of his phone lightly.

She blinked. Okay, that was a lot of zeroes. It was more money than she had earned in the last year. For a couple of days' work. It would pay for a good lawyer. Actually it would pay for the best lawyer in the country, she thought, her stomach knotting fiercely with relief and hope. It would mean she could keep her brothers from a life behind bars and how could she not want that? They had freed her from a different kind of prison, and yet this was a line she had never crossed or wanted to cross,

She shook her head. 'Even if I didn't get caught, I wouldn't be comfortable with what you're asking me to do.'

'Why?' There was a note in Harris Carver's voice that she couldn't place. 'Tiger McIntyre is no angel. From the outside, he looks like a winner but winning comes at a price. Yes, he's smart and determined, I'll give you that. He works hard but he also breaks the rules. Cuts corners. Crosses those lines that you're being so squeamish about. There is nothing he wouldn't do to get ahead. No one he wouldn't trample over to reach his goal. If you don't believe me, just read the Internet.'

He was telling the truth, she thought slowly, picturing Tiger McIntyre's intense, challenging gaze. McIntyre had a reputation for sidestepping laws and using any number of dubious tactics to get ahead. He took what he wanted and he got away with it because of his looks and his wealth and his power. Unlike her brothers, he never had to suffer the consequences of his actions. But maybe it was time he did.

'You don't need to feel bad about this, Ms Truitt. Believe me, this isn't the first time Tiger McIntyre has taken something of mine. But it will be the last,' Harris Carver said, leaning forward, and such was the venom in his voice that she had to press herself deep into the seat to stop herself from flinching.

Steadying her breathing, she cleared her throat. 'You said this was business, Mr Carver, but it's sounding awfully personal to me.'

There was a short, pulsing silence as he leaned back languidly against the cushions. 'Oh, it's personal, all right. You see, I know McIntyre is a thief, but he's picked the wrong person to steal from this time. So, first I want you to find what he stole, and get it back for me.' The grey eyes had narrowed on her face. 'And then I'm going to ruin him.'

Ten days later, Tiger McIntyre's private jet.

'So what was your gut feeling? Did we get it or not?'

Shifting back in his seat, Tiger McIntyre let the question from Nathan Park, his head of research and development, hang in the air. He knew the answer, of course. He always knew the answer. It was one of the reasons he had risen so far and so fast, turning his father's failed business into one of the front runners in the race for off-world mining.

It was a growing industry now, the exploration of the moon, but McIntyre was leading the race. Not just leading. Its AI-powered robots were lapping its rivals. Or all but one of them.

He tilted his head to let his gaze drift up past the endless blue of the stratosphere. Sometimes he dreamed about living on the moon. Of course, there would be negatives. But up there he would be able to just stop and pause for a moment, sit back and enjoy the view, because surely the demons that drove him ever onwards would be unable to follow into space.

But until then—

'On balance, yes.' He turned back towards Park, a slight smile pulling at his mouth. 'We have everything they want. Everything they need.'

In truth, there was only one other serious contender for this historic and extremely lucrative contract with the space agency. HCI. No surprise there, he thought, his lip curling. He and Harris Carver had been rivals for more than a decade now and their ongoing duel looked likely to extend into the foreseeable future and off-earth.

But then Harris had all the credentials. The college education, the astronaut father, the intergenerational cosmic bond. Whereas he had nothing.

Now was not the time to let Carver take up any more of his thoughts. In fact, he didn't want to think. Big meetings always made him horny as hell. It was that mix of adrenaline and testosterone. But currently he was in the usual state of being single so sex was out of the question, unless he could face calling one of his exes.

'Excuse me, Mr McIntyre.' It was the steward. 'Just to let you know that we will be landing in roughly twenty minutes so if you could fasten your seat belt.'

He nodded, but instead of buckling up, he reached for his phone and scrolled down the list of numbers. When he was younger, it had been different. Back then he had been happy just to casually hook up with women when he wanted sex.

He let his gaze drift back towards the window. Of course, that was no longer an option. He was too wealthy, too high profile. His security people would have a meltdown. So these days it was simpler to have a long-term but impermanent girlfriend. Although the friend part was a little inaccurate. He didn't do friends, female or male, not since college when he and Harris had fallen out big time and he had realised that trusting anyone, even someone you thought of as a brother, was riskier than firing a rocket into space. Although, truthfully, Harris had come late to that particular party. Watching his father's car crash of a love life over the best part of two decades had made it clear to him that the downside of relationships, particularly the romantic kind, was too high a price to pay.

But he was always upfront about what he wanted, which was exclusivity coupled with an understanding that the relationship was never going to end with an exchange of rings in front of witnesses.

And it worked. Okay, he only really saw them for sex and special events, but as his 'girlfriend' they got an entrée into his world and, besides, he always made his intentions clear from the beginning. It wasn't his fault that they assumed he would change or that it would be different with them.

Sometimes they got clingy, wanting him to meet their family or to get a place together, and that was a signal to end things. Other times, they would lose patience or their temper and break up with him. Either way, it wasn't a problem.

Usually.

But sometimes the timing was bad. Like now.

His hand tightened around the mobile. This year had been insane, in a good way. The business had doubled its profit in the first quarter and tripled it by the third. He had more than earned a vacation and typically he would head off to Italy, to his private island in the Venetian lagoon, and, in his opinion, September was the best month to visit. Temperatures were still warm but the summer glut of tourists had mostly left and Venice reverted to being the elusive, poetic city he loved.

And then there was the Regata Storica.

The *regata* was the social event of the year in the billionaires' social calendar. Coming hot on the heels of the Monaco Yacht Show, it started with a spectacular pageant on the waters of the famous lagoon and ended with the Colombina masked ball, which was the biggest charitable fundraising event in Europe. Graced by monarchs, heads of state, A-list celebrities and the top one per cent. It would be unthinkable not to attend, particularly as this year he was sponsoring a boat.

But to go alone would be even more unthinkable. For a man like him, a beautiful woman was as essential as an expensive watch or a pair of handmade shoes. It wasn't an ego thing. He didn't want or need anyone's approbation. It was more that perfection was intimidating. It kept people at arm's length and that was how he liked it.

Which left him with a problem.

Alexandra, the latest in his string of ex-girlfriends, was still seething at his decision to unceremoniously end things a few weeks ago. Frankly, though, he couldn't imagine asking her or any of his other exes anyway. Usually, he just asked whoever he was dating at the time, but if he invited them specifically then they would inevitably misread his intentions whatever he said.

What he needed was a woman who would behave like a girlfriend and then just walk away uncomplainingly. In other words, an escort, except he hadn't ever and would never pay a woman to be his date.

Face it, he told himself. *The woman you need doesn't*

exist and there is no point in hoping you're going to find her.

She was a creature of fantasy and, unlike his father, he was a man who dealt in facts, not feelings. And as he started to fasten his seat belt, he wondered once again if life might not be simpler on the moon.

Glancing up at the bank of clocks mounted on the wall opposite her desk, Sydney felt her heart accelerate. All of them showed different times. It was seven p.m. in Moscow, midnight in Beijing and five p.m. in London. Here in New York, it was only midday but the fact remained that she was running out of time. This was her last day working for the McIntyre Corporation and if she didn't deliver her end of the bargain to Harris Carver then she wouldn't get paid, and if she didn't get paid...

Her shoulders tensed against the back of her chair.

She could still hear the panic beneath the bravado in her brother Connor's voice when he'd called her from the police station. 'It's bad, Syd. They're saying it could be one to five years for all of us.' He paused, then cleared his throat. 'Including Tate.'

Selling and buying stolen car parts was not the worst crime in the world. But it was not her brothers' first offence. They had been in trouble since the day they could walk, always stupid stuff, avoidable stuff that made their mates laugh.

Until that day when she had called Connor on the phone she had stolen from ex-husband, Noah, and they had driven to Nevada to rescue her and ended up getting arrested for assault. They hadn't hurt Noah. They had wanted to, but, in the end, it was she who had pushed him. She was the one who had punched and kicked him. And in his fury and spite, he had accused them of assaulting him because he knew that would hurt her the most.

And she could have saved them then. She could have gone to the police and told them the truth, but she had been so ashamed of her bruises, so ashamed of her weakness, and her brothers had felt so guilty that they hadn't protected her, that they'd admitted to something that wasn't true. Which meant that thanks to her all three of them had a record for assault.

One to five years in jail. Connor would probably be okay. He was the oldest and knew how to handle himself. Her middle brother, Jimmy, had a smart mouth but he made people laugh so he might get by. But Tate...

Suddenly it was hard to breathe past the lump in her throat. Tate was the youngest of her three brothers. Just ten months older than her. They had been in the same year at school and she knew him inside out. Knew definitively that he wouldn't survive prison. All her brothers were magnets for trouble and not given to deep thinking, but Tate was softer than the others.

He couldn't go to prison. None of them could. And it was her responsibility to make sure they didn't. They had rescued her, saved her, in fact, and she was going to save them. But for that to happen, they needed a lawyer and not just the usual run-of-the-mill sort assigned by the court. She needed someone fierce and smart, which meant expensive. And that wouldn't be the only cost. If they managed by some miracle to avoid prison time, they would all be facing hefty fines.

Which was why she had taken this temping job at McIntyre.

Her gaze dropped to the ID badge hanging around her neck.

For her the hardest part wasn't having to live a lie. She had done that when she was with Noah. Kept the big secret of their marriage. It was just there was so much more riding on this than any other job. This was about more than money or her reputation as a white hat. It was about giving her brothers a second chance.

And you can do this, she told herself again. It was what she did every day for other businesses across the country. Tiptoeing her way around their cyber-security systems, using reverse-engineering malware to break down lines of code so that she could figure out how a virus worked and how to stop it.

Self-taught, she had worked hard to break into the industry and her business, Orb Weaver, was growing fast, and she wanted it to keep growing, which was why she had agreed to meet Carver in the first place.

And now she was working for the two biggest fish in the pond, only neither job was what she had imagined herself doing.

Gazing across the office to Tiger McIntyre's empty office, Sydney shivered. She still wasn't entirely sure that she had made the right choice. But she was here at the McIntyre headquarters off Fifth Avenue legitimately employed as an administrative assistant called Sierra Jones. And once she found the IP and returned to Carver, she would be paid. Far more money than was legitimately due for her services.

But then what she was doing wasn't exactly legitimate.

'You okay, Sierra?'

Her colleague, Abi, was staring at her uncertainly. 'You look like you've seen a ghost.'

She pasted a smile on her face. 'I'm fine. I just remembered I forgot to eat breakfast,' she lied.

Abi rolled her eyes. 'I always forget to eat lunch when *he's* in the building. I just get so nervous I'm going to mess up.'

There was no need to ask who 'he' was. He was the boss. Tiger McIntyre. Christened Tadhg but given his nickname because of his ferocious, single-minded pursuit of success, he was a man who had never encountered failure.

But Carver was right. He wasn't a good person.

She had done her research. If Tiger McIntyre had been Connor or Jimmy or Tate, he would have faced far stricter penalties and public censure for a whole bunch of things he'd done. Like when he'd failed to divulge the purchase of shares in a rival company within the required legal time limits. It seemed trivial until you realised that the delay saved him millions. Or, to put it another way, it cost the stockholders whose shares he'd bought that same amount.

Time and time again, McIntyre had got his way with regulators and officials through bravado and intimidation, often backed by his numerous supporters who made their allegiance known *en masse* via social media.

So how did *he* get away with it? Pursing her lips, Sydney tipped her head back slightly to gaze up at the ceiling so that the huge glass-walled office belonging to the CEO was no longer in eyeshot.

Easy. He was rich and powerful. He had people at his disposal who could spin the story so that all those boring regulators and boards with their incomprehensible titles were not gatekeepers of fair play but fussy, hair-splitting enemies of progress.

And now she was one of the people at his disposal.

Not that she had ever met Tiger McIntyre in person. That was the one positive. He was out of the office breaking rules in Zurich or London or Beijing and wasn't due back until after she left.

'Hi, Sierra.'

She looked up, glad for the distraction. This time it was Hannah. She was holding a tray with a covered plate, a glass and some cutlery wrapped in a napkin.

'You need to take this to him.'

'Him?' Sydney frowned. 'Who?'

'The boss, of course.'

The boss! Her stomach went into freefall. Later she would wonder whether it was stress or stupidity that made her question Hannah because obviously there was only one 'him'. Then again, it was an understandable mistake to make. Surely it was reasonable to expect some fanfare if Tiger McIntyre had arrived in the building?

'Sierra?' Now Hannah was frowning. 'Are you listening? Mr McIntyre is back and he wants you to take him his lunch, so if you wouldn't mind—'

She held out the tray.

Sydney stared at her, her heart rate picking up like one of her brothers' souped-up cars. He must know something. A man as important as he wouldn't ordinarily even notice someone like her. Or was having to lead a double life just making her see threats where there were none? It was hard to say. All she knew for sure was that with every passing hour she was feeling more on edge, like an antelope leaping out of its skin every time it heard a twig snap.

She cleared her throat. 'Why does he want me to take it in?' It was one thing working here, quite another to walk into the lion's den.

'What?' Hannah frowned. 'I don't know. Maybe he can see how busy the rest of us are? Just put it on his desk.' She jerked her head towards the towering drinks fridge. 'And take a bottle of mineral water in too. Still, not sparkling. Get one from the back. He likes it well chilled.'

'Should I say something to him?'

Hannah looked horrified. 'No, absolutely not. Oh, and don't touch anything.'

There was no escape, and during the short walk to Tiger McIntyre's office her panic intensified, not helped by the glimpse she caught of herself in the glass of his door. She looked flustered and nervous.

Not that it mattered. It wasn't as if she were here to seduce McIntyre. Wasn't looking to seduce anyone, period.

Taking a breath, Sydney tapped lightly on the door and pushed it open. At first, she thought the huge office was empty, but then she saw him. He was standing at the window, reading something on his phone, and as she stared at his back, her breath caught in her throat and she felt a ripple of panic and guilt scuttle down her spine in the same way it did whenever she saw the blue and white flashing lights of a police car glide past her family home.

But why should she feel guilty? Okay, legally what she was doing was dubious but in essence she was righting a wrong. For all his fancy tailoring and handmade shoes, this man was a bigger criminal than her brothers. All she was doing was helping to expose that.

Keeping her eyes focused straight ahead, she walked swiftly across the room. She slid the plate onto his desk, and then, holding her breath, she unscrewed the bottle and poured out a glass of water.

'We haven't met, have we?'

It was a simple enough question, but Sydney felt the back of her neck prickle at the sound of the deep, masculine voice, and she turned sharply towards its owner.

For a moment, all she could do was stare. Her heart beat in her throat and her skin seemed suddenly too tight and hot, because Tiger McIntyre was no longer just a photo on her laptop, he was here in the flesh, all six feet three inches of him.

'No, we haven't. I only started two days ago.' She watched mutely as he began to walk towards her.

'What's your name?' he said, pocketing his phone.

'Sierra,' she said quickly. 'Sierra Jones.'

As if to expose the lie, the name, which she had chosen because it shared the first syllable with her own, crackled like popping candy on her tongue and her stomach fluttered as he looked at her closely, narrowed eyes appraising her in a way that made her feel as though he were looking beneath her skin, seeing into her soul.

Under any other circumstances it wouldn't have been a comfortable feeling.

But she barely noticed because she was still reeling from the shock of his beauty. Although it shouldn't have been a shock because she already knew what he looked like. Even before she had done her research, scouring the Internet for stories of his unscrupulous and line-blurring behaviour, his face had been familiar, but she had assumed the pictures she'd seen of him had been edited to flatter or that the camera had caught him on a good day.

But the truth was that none of the images she had seen did him justice. His face was arrestingly, astonishingly beautiful with a clean jawline and high sculpted cheekbones that would grace the pages of any Renaissance artist's sketchbook. And those eyes—

On her laptop, they looked light brown, but in person and up close, they were gold like the sun, only they lacked the sun's warmth. Instead, they were hard and glittering and unreadable.

Her own eyes skated across his face. Everything about him was hard, uncompromising, even his mouth. And yet for some reason there was something undeniably sensual about the shape of his lips, so that even though they were currently set in a line she could imagine them softening to fit against hers. The thought made her heart jerk forward and, to cover her reaction, she held out her hand.

'I'm not permanent. I'm covering for Maddie.'

As his eyes locked on hers, she swore silently. What was she doing? She was supposed to be keeping her head down. Not drawing attention to herself.

'I see,' he said slowly, taking her hand in what must surely be a reflex action, but as his fingers wrapped around hers she felt a sharp shock like electricity and she jerked free of his grip.

'Sorry, it's static,' she said quickly. 'I get it sometimes from the keyboard.'

He stared at her for so long that she thought she had

missed his reply, but then he said in that same smooth, deep voice, 'Are you enjoying working here?'

'Yes.' Smiling slightly, she nodded, because it wasn't a total lie. She liked her colleagues and, if things were different, she might have enjoyed being Sierra for real, aside from the heels. Walking in them required the use of muscles she hadn't known she had and it was a miracle she hadn't broken her neck. But like the manicure and the designer handbag, they were part of her Sierra costume. And she would be glad to go back to being herself. Leading a double life was giving her sleepless nights. Frankly, she would be happy when five o'clock came and she would be able to put this chapter of her life behind her and get her life and, more importantly, her brothers' lives back on track.

She owed them that. Owed them her freedom, and a life lived without fear.

She nodded. 'Everyone here has been very kind and helpful.'

Two tiny lines formed a crease in the centre of his forehead and his burnished gaze got more intense. 'You're a long way from home, Ms Jones.'

Her stomach lurched sideways like a boat hit by a rogue wave. 'I'm sorry—' She tried to keep the panic out of her voice but she felt it wash over her anyway.

'California, isn't it?'

How did he know that? She lifted a hand to her suddenly pounding heart, feeling the trap snap shut.

His mouth tugged up minutely at one corner. 'We have a research and development test site up in the hills so I've spent a lot of time there and I recognised your accent. I'm guessing San Francisco.'

As relief flooded her, she managed to make her smile stay in place. 'Los Angeles.'

'Ah, the city of angels,' he said slowly. 'Ever visited New York before?' As she shook her head, his gaze moved past her to his desk and then back to her face. 'May I?'

His grip didn't hurt but when it came to physical contact she liked to be in control. Only she was still dizzy and off balance from this sudden breach of her invisibility, so when he took her elbow and steered her towards the window, she didn't pull away the way she normally did when someone touched her without warning or permission.

She could feel the calluses on his fingers, so that story about him working in the mines was true. For some reason that surprised her. She had thought it was just spin, propaganda designed to reinforce his status as the ordinary working man made good.

'This is the only way to see New York,' he said softly, and then he let go of her arm and she felt suddenly confused and angry because for the first time in years she hadn't minded being touched. On the contrary, she could feel herself leaning into his orbit, and her skin was quivering, itching to feel the warm, firm grip of his fingers again.

And not just on her arm.

Her pulse was a smooth, dizzying drum roll of panic and something else. Something deeper, more dangerous. Something she couldn't name. But it didn't need a name, apparently, to make her breath back up in her throat and her mind go blank as if everything she knew were gone, lost, forgotten, irrelevant. As if this was the moment when her life started. And although she knew that was absurd, she also knew it was true.

'So why did you leave LA? Was it a whim or did you have a particular reason?'

Yes, she thought. His name was Noah and he had almost broken her. He had taken her away from her family and friends. First to a flat and then to a tiny, isolated house far from any neighbours.

Far enough that nobody would hear her screams.

She still had the scars from their time together, although his cruelty had not been restricted to physical violence, so some were not ever visible. The bruises from when she had exhausted his patience and he had twisted her arm until she'd thought it would snap, they had faded. The hair he had pulled out had grown back.

There was one burn mark on her arm that had faded to a dull sheen and, of course, the implant she wore to replace the tooth he had knocked out, but it was the scars beneath the surface that had lingered longest and had left the most damage. That quiet rage that was always with her. Rage and a stifling shame at having been that woman. There was fear too that it could happen again. That she hadn't seen the signs then or had wilfully chosen to ignore them. And not understanding why she had let that happen meant that it could happen again.

Noah and the fear his name provoked was the reason she hadn't dated in five years.

'No, not really,' she lied. 'I just wanted a change of scenery.'

For a moment, his molten eyes rested on her face and she had that same strange feeling that he was seeing inside her head, and she felt a rush of panic. She had never planned on meeting Tiger in person, but now she was in his office, making polite chit-chat with him while lying to his face and stealing from him. It was both surreal and nerve-racking. Every word felt charged, and she was terrified she was going to give herself away.

'Well,' she said stiffly after a taut, electric moment she didn't understand but felt everywhere. 'I should probably be getting back.' But she didn't move, didn't look away from him even though she knew that she should because it was this man, it was him, Tiger McIntyre. He was making her feel this way. Making her drop her guard, making her ache—

'Of course. Don't let me keep you from your work.' He was already turning away. 'Oh, just for the record. My preference is for undressed.'

'Sorry.' She blinked as his gaze arrowed in on her in a way that made her body feel taut and loose at the same time.

'The salad. They've put dressing on it. I prefer it without.'

Her heart had somehow shifted to her throat, and she stared at him, trying to breathe around it. Was this for real? Did he actually care about his salad? Or was he just making conversation to keep her here? She felt another flicker of panic. Focus, she told herself. Focus on why you're here. Who you're doing it for.

'Sorry, I didn't know. Would you like me to get you another one?'

But before he could reply, his phone started to ring and he retrieved it from his pocket and switched from English to what sounded like Japanese. His eyes shuttered and he turned away and, recognising dismissal, she turned and walked swiftly out of his office.

For the rest of the day, she kept one eye on her computer screen and the other on the door to Tiger McIntyre's office. Throughout the afternoon, there was a revolving door of suited executives arriving and leaving his office. Occasionally she would catch a glimpse of the man they had all come to see and she would force her gaze back to her computer.

At some point, Hannah had come over to show her the pictures from her wedding-dress fitting. Staring down at the slideshow of frothy white dresses, Sydney had suddenly felt her skin on her face warm without reason and, glancing up, she had almost bitten the inside of her cheek as her eyes had collided with the shimmering gold gaze of Tiger McIntyre and she had felt that same jolt as before, only this time he hadn't even been touching her.

Not her, Sierra, she'd told herself quickly. As Sydney, she disapproved of Tiger. His behaviour. His abuse of privilege and power. As Sydney, she would never feel that strange, ungovernable pull of yearning or wonder.

After that she had kept her focus steady on her screen.

Not that it had mattered. It appeared that quietly and without her permission something inside her had turned itself towards him.

She was switching between screens now. The first was for the work she was doing as Sierra Jones, but she had a second incognito screen where she was working through the list of images, searching for the digital fingerprint that Harris Carver had sent her of his IP. It had taken her less than five hours to bypass the firewalls, but the fingerprint had offered not one image but nine hundred and fifty-three.

It was fine. She had come up with a workaround that had reduced that number to just under two hundred. So, assuming there was no other glitch, she would be walking out of here at five-thirty p.m. Then all she had to do was hand over the flash drive to Carver. It was a bit old school but it would leave no trail. Or not one that could be traced back to him.

Glancing up, she scanned the desks. The office was surprisingly empty this evening. Yesterday and the day before there had been quite a few people hanging around but tonight it was just her.

And Tiger McIntyre.

Her pulse twitched as she glanced over at his office to where she could just see his outline dark against the fading light. It was as if her eyes were being pulled to him by some magnetic force and, gritting her teeth, she glanced back down at the computer and switched screens again. Please be done, she prayed silently. But there were still ninety images to go.

Why was it taking so long? Her hands were clammy and her fingers felt fat and clumsy as she picked up her phone and her water bottle and slid them into her bag.

How much time did she have left before she had to be out of the building?

When she glanced up again, her heart stopped beating. Just stopped.

Tiger McIntyre had left his office and was walking towards her and there was something purposeful about him, an intensity of focus that made her pull out the flash drive as a tiny flicker of foreboding snaked down her spine. In one smooth movement, she pocketed it, shut down the screen and got to her feet and, stomach somersaulting, she made her way between the desks to the elevator.

'Come on, come on,' she murmured, her heart a dark thud against her ribs, pressing the button frantically. But it was too late. A shadow blocked the light and she turned to find Tiger McIntyre standing beside her, the dark gold gleam of his gaze rooting her to the spot.

'Sierra, I need you to come with me.' There was a warning edge of steel to the softness in his voice and she couldn't breathe for a moment. 'You and I are going to have a little chat.'

To his left, she could see the exit sign for the staircase and it was almost impossible to stop herself from ducking under his arm and making a bolt for safety.

Not that there was such a thing for her any more, she realised in that moment with a shiver. Once an apex predator caught its prey, the chances of escape were somewhere between remote and zero.

'Is there a problem?' she said, trying not to sound as panicky as she felt.

He didn't reply.

He didn't need to. The hard curve to his mouth and the two security guards hovering discreetly against the walls did it for him. Instead, he jerked his thumb in the direction of his office. That was the last place on earth she wanted to be but what choice did she have? And after a moment she turned and began to walk back the way she had come, only this time with Tiger following a pace behind, his golden gaze boring into her back, muscular body moving with the smooth, silent, slow-motion grace of his namesake.

CHAPTER TWO

AS THEY REACHED his office, Tiger sidestepped past her, dragging a chair in his wake and dumping it in front of his desk.

'Sit,' he said coolly, and that coolness surprised him because inside his fury was churning like white-hot magma. It was astonishing to him that this was even happening. His firewalls were the stuff of legend, as complex and intractable to unravel as a Gordian knot, but Sydney had somehow hacked his server. But even more astonishing than that was the fact that she was currently masquerading as an employee.

How had this happened? To him? He was not easily duped, particularly by women, but earlier when she'd come into his office, he'd actually thought that his head of IT had made a mistake. Nobody that young could be so nerveless. In part that was why he'd wanted her to bring him his lunch—so that he could meet her in person before he confronted her. Only then he'd got distracted by that soft mouth of hers and the pale curve of her jaw. The same jaw that was currently tilting up defiantly in his general direction.

'You know, actually, I don't think I will. You see, I don't

work for you any more. My contracted hours ended three minutes ago so—'

He watched as she took a step back, but as she turned towards the exit one of the huge security guards moved in front of the doorway to block her escape.

Tiger held up his hand. 'Thanks, Carlos. I can take it from here. I'll let you know when I need you.'

There was a soft but final-sounding click as Carlos closed the door.

'You're not going anywhere,' he said, letting the warning in his words extend to his glittering gold gaze. 'Like I said, you and I need to have a talk.'

'I don't know what this is about but—' she began, but he cut her off.

'You know exactly what this is about. But I'm happy to spell it out. You hacked my system and you stole from me. So why don't you stop with the whole wide-eyed, first-time-in-New-York act and take a seat? And then I suggest you start talking.'

She sat down with such bad grace that it made him want to frogmarch her down to the police station himself. And yet a part of him was captivated by her and the strange, seductive tension between them and this verbal sparring that felt almost like foreplay.

What the—?

He swore silently, caught off guard by the inappropriateness of that thought and, blanking his mind to the pulse of heat beating a slow drum roll down his linea alba, he leaned back against the desk, stretching his long legs out in front of him.

'You've made a mistake.'

His gaze didn't flicker. 'I don't make mistakes.' He wasn't boasting. He was careful, tediously so, and he was happy to exploit any loophole that served his purpose, but the last time he'd been wrongfully accused of something, he'd ended up getting kicked out of university, so he didn't make mistakes.

The memory of Harris's cold-eyed contempt made him feel suddenly adrift, and, hating it still had the power over him, he focused his frustration on the woman sitting in front of him.

'You, on the other hand, have racked up quite a few in the last few days. Although I prefer to give them their correct title, which is criminal offences. There's gaining unauthorised access to a computer system. Stealing data, presumably with the intention of selling it on to a third party. Industrial espionage. But I'm no lawyer so I'm sure that's just the tip of the iceberg.'

That was better, he thought, feeling a sharp stab of satisfaction as her face stilled. 'What?' His eyes held hers as he deliberately let his mouth pull into a shape that could only be described as mocking.

'Did you think you're the first? 'Fraid not. You're certainly not the best,' he said softly, but with a hint of malice because he wanted to punish her, to wound her pride. Watching her pupils flare, he knew that he'd hit his target.

'It's not quite an everyday occurrence but I get a lot of people trying to mess me over.'

Sydney glared at him. 'If this is how you behave, I can well believe it.'

He stared down at her, his gaze bright and steady, his mouth a contemptuous curl, but he could feel the spark of her defiance igniting a flame he didn't normally feel and shouldn't be feeling because this woman, this red-haired vixen who had done more than any man would dare to do, she should be apologising at least or, better still, be on her knees begging for mercy.

A burst of heat, astonishing in its intensity, surged through his veins as his brain offered up all manner of possible reasons for her to be kneeling in front of him that he didn't want to acknowledge with Sydney here in the room.

'The difference with you is that I don't normally have the pleasure of meeting them face to face.'

She held his gaze. 'For the last time, I don't know what you're talking about. Look, I'm a hard worker but I do have to get up from my computer sometimes, and there're people coming and going all day. Any one of them could have done whatever it is you think I did.'

He heard her breath go shallow as his gaze narrowed on her. 'I don't think you did it, I know you did. I have proof. So do you, actually. It's in your bag.' Now, he held out his hand. 'Give it to me.'

'What? No.' Her fingers tightened around the handle of her bag. Her pulse was beating a wild staccato in her throat and just for a second there she had looked scared, and far too young to be sparring with a man like him.

But she had brought this on herself.

'I'm not going to ask again.'

She gave a small, taut laugh. 'Let me guess. This is where you threaten me. Where you tell me that we can do this the easy way or the hard way.'

His eyes met hers. 'Easy's not on the table. Just hard, and harder.'

'There's nothing in my bag.'

'Then you won't mind me taking a look inside.'

'Not if you don't mind me hurling it at your head first,' she snapped back as if he were the one at fault here, and for a moment he was stunned and furious all over again that she should talk to him that way, and yet for some reason he also wanted to laugh.

He settled for shrugging. 'Not the most sensible of responses unless you're looking to add assault to your list of crimes.'

She drew a breath, and he could see she was trying to maintain her composure. 'I haven't committed any crimes,' she said firmly, her eyes fixed on his as she stalked past him and upended her bag and shook it, scattering the contents across his desk. As she tossed the bag at him, her face gave nothing away but he was looking for a flash drive, not remorse, and, taking his time, he sifted through the detritus on his desk before checking the interior of the bag.

'Happy?' she said as his eyes found hers.

'Not yet. But I will be. Empty your pockets, Sydney,' he ordered, pushing away from the desk, and maybe there was something wrong with him, but he found he very nearly enjoyed the small, sharp intake of breath that followed his instruction.

Sydney's chin jerked up, not only because Tiger had got to his feet but because he had used her real name. She stared back at him, panic lifting her up and throwing her down like a dark rushing tide, pulling her under and sweeping her out into the ocean.

She had thought she'd been careful, ultra careful, but

normally she was the one looking for the intruder. Not the intruder herself.

'Not a nice feeling, is it? Having people upend your life?' he said softly, so softly that for a moment her brain actually got confused and thought that he was backing off. But then that mouth of his twisted into a smile that made her understand that she was in trouble. Made her understand on a stomach-churning, visceral level just how ruthless he was.

Sydney held her breath. It didn't really change anything, but part of the reason she'd been just about holding it together was because she could tell herself that this was happening to Sierra. Now it was happening to her. Now it felt real.

All of it.

Blood rushed to her cheeks as she remembered that strange weightless feeling when he took hold of her arm, and that longing to get closer—

'How did you find out my name?' she said hoarsely.

He gestured towards the ID tag. 'I called in a favour. An ex-secret service friend of mine ran a facial recognition check and your driver's licence came up. You're Sydney Truitt. You live in Los Angeles and you're the CEO of Orb Weaver, a cyber-security company. A little detail that, oddly, you chose not to put on your CV.'

'It wasn't relevant,' she said as calmly as she could, fixing her gaze at a point to the left of his shoulder.

He didn't respond for a moment and she tried telling herself that it didn't get to her, but inevitably, as she knew it would, her head turned towards him of its own accord. There was a look of dark impatience on his face.

'If you say so. What is relevant is that, approximately

seventeen hours ago, my head of IT picked up some un-usual out-of-hours activity on your CPU.'

This was the worst-case scenario. She felt her stomach drop. It was a quiet program but she'd had to keep it running day and night.

'They check, you see, and it was low-level, just working quietly away in the background, but your machine was doing something it shouldn't. I'll let you have a few moments to come up with a reason why that was happening, but in the meantime, you can empty your pockets. Oh, and let me be clear—if you don't, I will ask Carlos to do it for you,' he added.

He would do it as well. This was not a man who made empty threats.

She had been cornered before so many times in the past by a different angry man and back then she'd tried to placate, to distract, tried to make herself small because she had been too scared to stand up to him.

Only for some reason she wasn't afraid of this man. Not physically anyway.

Still, though, she felt goosebumps spread across her skin as his glittering, disdainful gaze narrowed on her face. But she couldn't crack now. If she kept her head there was a chance she could front this out. Her throat tightened. She had to front it out.

Reaching into her pocket, she pulled out the flash drive and put it onto the palm of his hand. For a moment he stared at her assessingly, as if she were an animal in a trap and he were deciding how best to put her out of her misery.

'Is that it?'

She nodded.

He turned it over between his fingers. 'I know what you've taken. My question is what you were planning on doing with it. Because we both know that you weren't doing this for fun.'

Sydney breathed out shakily. For a moment she considered telling Tiger that it wasn't her idea. That she had been hired by Harris Carver to do his dirty work. But, really, what would be the point of giving up his name? Carver would deny all knowledge of their meeting and she had no proof.

Except her word, and right now she was pretty sure that wouldn't count for much.

Now it was her turn to shrug. 'Actually, I was. It's what people like me do,' she lied. 'We like the challenge and it's kind of like a hobby, seeing if we can get into a system. And I can see why that might upset you.'

'Is that an apology? Because you might need to work on it a little.'

'You're just sore because I beat your firewalls.'

He looked at her levelly. 'I'm sore because you lied to me and because you tried to steal from me at the same time as taking a salary from me.'

In the past, with Noah, she was always having to defend herself against untrue accusations and at the time she had often thought it would be fairer if she had done the things he'd claimed. But now she discovered that it wasn't a comfortable feeling being accused of something she *had* done, however justifiably.

She took a step forward, her hands balling by her sides. 'I don't steal.'

'Is something getting lost in translation? Because typically stealing is when you take someone else's property without permission.' The sarcastic note in his voice was like a steel scraping against the flint of her temper and she felt a spark catch fire.

'If you'd let me finish,' she snapped. 'What I was trying to say was that I don't steal from people who don't deserve it.'

'Right, because you're just a gender-flipped modern-day Robin Hood.' He didn't roll his eyes. There was no need. 'You're delusional.'

'And you're a hypocrite.' She was practically shouting now, her voice shaking with an anger that was only partially aimed at Tiger but she let it roll through her. 'You make me sick. You break the rules all the time.'

She felt the fury in her words bang into him and bounce away harmlessly because this man was not some soft-handed, Ivy League trust-fund baby. Tiger McIntyre had worked in the mines before he'd pushed his business into the big time. It was going to take more than a few insults to make him back off. Most likely it would take some very big sticks and stones. Boulders perhaps.

'Rules, not laws. Nothing I do is illegal.'

She shook her head, her fury giving way to panic now, because she was running out of options, out of words. She could feel the trap closing around her.

'Just because you haven't been punished doesn't mean you shouldn't be. But you're rich enough to bully and buy your way out of trouble.'

'You don't know anything about me,' he said softly.

'And you don't know anything about me,' she retorted.

'I know you're a hacker, and that you think that makes you different from other criminals, you know, the ones that rob stores and steal cars.'

'I've never stolen anything. This is the first time I—'

He shook his head. 'Even if that were true, what difference does it make? You're still just a thief.'

Tiger watched her eyebrows lift into cool, delicate arcs.

'Well, at least I don't get my kicks from playing judge, jury and executioner.'

He didn't know what he'd expected when he'd stalked back into his office with Sydney. Tears maybe. Possibly hysterics. The contents of her bag hurled in his face. But not this defiance, this bravado, this cat-and-mouse wordplay that was entirely irrelevant and extraneous, and yet for some reason he was enjoying it. Enjoying her and the feeling of having her right where he wanted her.

Not that she would admit to that.

Not yet, anyway.

'You have quite a mouth on you, Ms Truitt,' he said at last. 'Lots of opinions. Lots of accusations. Just not much in the way of cold, hard facts. But I pay my taxes so I guess I can leave it to the police to find those out.'

Sydney stared at him, her face stilling as if his words had cast a spell over her. If he hadn't been watching her covertly since lunchtime, he might not even have noticed the slight quiver to her body as if she was having to hold herself together not just metaphorically but literally.

He felt something pinch inside him.

He had been telling the truth when he'd said that this wasn't the first time his company had been hacked. For any major business, institution or high-profile celebrity it was a constant threat. Some hackers did it for the rush. Some liked the challenge of defeating a worthy opponent. Others did it for the chaos they caused, or simply the money. All had a willingness to break the law.

But, for all her defiance, this woman didn't strike him as being some kind of disrupter. In truth, she seemed altogether too young to be playing games with people like him. And yet there was a wariness in her eyes that didn't match her age, a tautness to her shoulders as if she were waiting for the sky to fall on her.

Only surely it already had. This was it. The end of the world. Disaster not averted. A real-life elimination event involving her reputation.

It didn't make any sense.

Then again, nothing about this woman or how she made him react made any kind of sense. Why, for example, when he should be focusing on the fact that he had caught her red-handed hacking his system, was he so aware of that curl of dark red hair that had come loose from the riotous mass of dark copper strands twisted into a low ponytail? Why could he not tear his gaze away from where it now lay coiled in a question mark over her right breast?

That he was even thinking about her hair, much less her breast, was just one of many things that had happened today that Tiger McIntyre didn't understand. First there had been the moment earlier when she'd walked, no, sashayed into his office with his lunch. Women walked in and out of his office all day every day and normally he barely registered them, but for some reason Sydney had made him stop reading his emails.

He swore silently. And not just any old email. An email from the United States space administrator no less.

But as he'd looked up and caught sight of her reflection in the glass that hadn't seemed to matter. And he had watched her in silence, waiting for her to acknowledge him, confused at his uncharacteristic behaviour because he never watched or waited for any woman.

And they always acknowledged him first, even the ones who thought they were playing hard to get.

But she hadn't.

Because she was a thief, he told himself irritably. Probably she couldn't meet his eye because she was hacking into his accounts, stealing his IP.

Only that wasn't true. She had met his eye. His chest tightened, remembering the gleam of her irises. Espresso brown. That was the colour of her eyes, and as their gazes had locked, he'd felt his heart accelerate and every single nerve ending start to shiver just as if he'd downed several black coffees in quick succession. It had sideswiped him and he'd been completely shaken by the burst of heat and need that had roared through him, so much so that he had taken her arm as if it were the most normal thing in the world to do.

Shaking his head free of that memory, he took a step towards her. 'What did you think was going to happen? That you'd get a dressing-down and then I'd let you walk out of here? This doesn't go away. This only gets worse.'

She was staring past him into the darkness. 'I didn't get that far.'

That made no sense either. Sydney was clearly smart. Smart enough to create a false employment record and get herself hired by the temp agency. Smart enough to hack past the McIntyre firewalls.

And yet he believed her.

'Maybe you should have done, because you accessed my private server without authorisation. You've stolen intellectual property presumably for profit. You're looking at time in a federal prison.'

'No.' Now her eyes found his. She was shaking her head and her voice sounded thin, as if she was finding it hard to speak, but he told himself that he didn't care, that she deserved to feel like that. 'I can't go to prison. I have commitments, responsibilities—'

'You mean a child?'

It was as if he'd been kicked in the chest by a horse. Which was ridiculous. She was a stranger. He had clapped eyes on her for the first time today. More importantly, she was a liar and a thief, and yet the thought of her having had a baby with some man that wasn't him scraped against something inside him.

'No. That's not what I mean. I have bills to pay.'

He felt a rush of relief, sharp and so incomprehensible that it was swiftly replaced by anger. With her, with himself and, as usual, with his father. Because there was no day when he didn't feel angry with his father.

His teeth were on edge, his body so tense now that he thought it might fly apart. 'You should have thought about that before you took me on.' It was out of his hands. There were laws. She had broken them.

'I could work for you.'

He frowned. Her beautiful dark eyes were narrowed on his face and there was a faint tremor beneath her skin.

'You? Work for me.' He repeated the words as if he couldn't believe that he'd heard them correctly, although he knew that his hearing was perfect. 'You think I'd trust *you* to work for me? After this?' He laughed then, showing his teeth, although it was a laugh without a hint of mirth. 'I don't do second chances, Ms Truitt. You cross me once, we're done.'

'I got past your firewall,' she said after a hard pause, and there was a flush to her cheeks. 'That shouldn't have happened. I can make sure it doesn't happen again.'

'An argument which might have more power if you hadn't been caught.' Why was he even having this conversation? He should just let the police deal with her, and, in the meantime, Carlos could babysit her.

And yet, he couldn't quite bring himself to do that, and he didn't understand why. He just knew that at some point in their conversation he had drifted closer to her. Too close. Close enough that he could touch her if he wanted to. Which, in spite of what she had done, he did.

His eyes rested on her flushed face, then dropped to the curve of her mouth.

Such a thing had never happened before and knowing that this woman was the reason, that she was causing this uncharacteristic reaction, made him feel more tense than he'd ever felt. He wasn't that man; had never wanted to be the kind of man who let his need for a woman dictate his behaviour.

His jaw tightened. Unsurprisingly, given that ever since he was four years old he'd watched his father make a total fool of himself with women, watched him confuse lust with love. Gerry McIntyre could casually mention a woman's name over breakfast one day and the next he would have proposed to her.

It was a pattern that had repeated itself over twenty years and cost his father a fortune. By the time Tiger took over following his father's premature death at fifty-nine, the medium-sized mining business Gerry had inherited from his father had been whittled away, hollowed out to fund his multiple divorces. All that had remained was the name, a whole heap of debt and a bunch of unpaid, understandably unhappy employees. Oh, and some very rich former wives.

Not substitute mothers, none even attempting to be. He had been nothing to them. Just a rival pull on his father's time. Not that his father had needed much pulling. Whenever he'd fallen in love, Gerry had been like a blinkered horse galloping for the finishing line.

Tiger had so longed for his father's attention. And there had been times when Gerry would remember he had a son, like when he'd wanted to watch the game. Mostly, though, Tiger had been easily forgotten, a lonely little boy who'd had to be self-reliant to survive. Who'd grown up to become a solitary, elusive man.

Because he wasn't like his father. He had no intention of marrying one woman, let alone six. As for letting Sydney Truitt near his business, forget it. He'd seen his father lose too much from trusting the wrong people. He preferred to put his faith in the evidence to hand and, on that basis, Sydney was not someone he could trust.

His gaze moved to where she stood a few feet away. Anyone else in her position would be pleading by now, or need restraining by the security guards, but there was a stillness to her as she waited for his next move and he found himself admiring her composure.

What the—?

Clearly, he needed a break more urgently than he'd thought if he was starting to admire someone he'd just caught stealing from him. He was obviously suffering from nervous exhaustion. Only, from somewhere at the margins of his mind, an idea was taking shape. Briefly, he tested it for weakness.

But it was sound. Pragmatic. A near-perfect solution to a problem that he had shelved on the flight back to New York.

It was also completely insane, he told himself.

Or was it? In business, if you had your rival over a metaphorical barrel, you took what you wanted, what you needed, and right now he needed a no-strings partner. But just because Sydney would be given access to his private life, it didn't mean that it was personal. This was a transaction like any other.

'You react well to pressure,' he said after a moment.

She stared at him, those brown eyes confused, but curious. Because his non sequitur had piqued her interest. And that in turn had piqued his. Curiosity, the desire to know more and so be more, that he understood. More than understood, he thought, remembering the first time his father had taken him to the copper mine in Colorado. It had propelled him forward, given him wings.

The need to have control over what was his. To not have to sit by, powerless to intervene as it slipped through his fingers, that was the engine that drove him onwards, but his curiosity was the fuel.

'Yes.' As she nodded, the slight movement of her head

made another curl slip free of its moorings and watching its progress made him feel light-headed.

'It's part of the job. If you get emotional then you lose focus.'

True, he thought, dragging his eyes away from the distracting curl back to her face. Only that didn't help because now the part of his brain that should be cool and clinical was distracted by the freckles on her face.

She had beautiful skin, smooth and pale aside from a faint flush of pink along her cheekbones, so a perfect canvas for that mesmerising sprinkling of sun kisses. A beat of heat danced along his limbs. Was that all there were or were there others elsewhere?

'That's good to know,' he said, shutting the door on that thought. 'You see, while we've been talking, I've realised I have got a use for you after all. A short-term contract.'

He watched as her shoulders dropped fractionally. 'You won't regret it. I can start tomorrow.' She hesitated. 'But I'll need some kind of security clearance to get into the building. My pass expired today.'

He let her wait, as she had made him wait earlier in the day, liking how it made the colour in her cheeks spread like spilt wine.

Finally, he shook his head. 'You won't need a pass. I don't want you anywhere near my office. But you will need a passport.'

Her forehead creased. 'Where do you want me to go?'

My bed, he thought, his body suddenly hot and tight.

Without the pants, but she could keep that blouse on. His gaze dropped to her spiked heels. And those shoes. It was a cliché, but clichés became clichés because they spoke to something true.

But not enough to act on. Coming to his senses, he met her gaze. 'Venice,' he said slowly. 'That's where I want you to go. Where you need to be.'

'You have an office in Venice?'

'No, I don't. And I don't need your hacking skills. I have a big event coming up. In Venice. I need a date, a girlfriend of sorts. Just for a week.'

She was looking at him as if he had lost his mind, and to be fair a part of him was thinking exactly the same.

'Is this your idea of a joke?' Her eyes clashed with his, the pupils wide with shock and outrage. 'Because it's not funny.'

'It's not a joke. It's a proposition. A chance for you to avoid a prison term. I'm sure you're familiar with the concept. You see it a lot in the movies. Bunch of no-good criminals are offered freedom and a pardon if they take on a dangerous mission. I believe it's called the "boxed crook" trope.'

She let out a small, brittle laugh. 'And there I was thinking you were just being a typical male sleazebag taking advantage of a situation to get his leg over.'

The mouth on her! Tiger stared down at Sydney, feeling his hackles rise. 'For the record, I don't take advantage of women, Ms Truitt. And in any case, you don't need to worry. I'm very choosy about who I get my leg over.'

'Then I suggest you "choose" some other woman,' she said, and there was an edge to her voice that made him think his words had hit their target. 'There must be one in New York who would enjoy your company.'

'Many,' he said coolly. 'But I can't think of another woman who shares your unique skill set. You see, I need someone who understands that our "relationship" is just for show. Someone who can play a part under pressure. Persuade people that she's something she's not. Lie to their faces.' His eyes locked with hers. 'Someone willing and available to bend to my will.'

Her pupils flared. 'Then you definitely need to choose another woman because I'm neither of those things.'

Watching her face, Tiger wondered what it was exactly about this woman that drew him to her so intensely. It was maddening to feel this way, but to not understand why.

Most likely it was just this whole set-up, he reassured himself. He was intrigued, or maybe that wasn't the right way to describe how he was feeling but he couldn't think of a better one.

'You misunderstand me, Sydney.' He saw her hands ball into fists as he used her name. 'When I said willing and available, I meant within the context of the alternative being jail time.'

CHAPTER THREE

PUT LIKE THAT, she had no choice, Sydney thought, panic scrabbling in her throat. But, of course, she'd never had one because the choice was between two equally unpalatable options. The classic rock or hard place. Deep blue sea and the devil.

Remembering Noah's twisted face as he'd reeled off her faults in that cold, hissing voice, she shivered. In some ways, too many ways right now, Tiger had more power over her than Noah had ever had. And yet, although he was making her feel nervous and tenser than she'd ever felt, that wasn't the same thing as being scared.

The worst part was that she had chosen Noah. There had been no threat hanging over her. At eighteen she had found his authority and rigour thrillingly exotic. He had been so unlike her family, so articulate and emphatic, and she had been hooked.

Had put herself on the hook, she thought, throat tightening at her naivety. *No*, not naivety. To be naive was to be credulous and clueless about how the world worked. But she was a Truitt, she knew how it worked and, more importantly, how often it failed to work. She had been stupid and smug, believing herself to be different, better than everyone around her. And she had been better academically. She'd worked hard and she'd liked school. There had been rules to follow, and she'd found it relaxing to know what she had to do and where she had to be at what time.

Because home had been far from relaxing. It had been chaotic and overwhelming, and she'd always been on edge, always worrying about what was going to happen next. Noah had seen that, and exploited it, flattering her and isolating her and telling her 'hard truths'; telling her she deserved better.

Now she could see that his 'honesty' and principles were a mask for his cruel, controlling nature, but back then she had wanted to believe him so badly that she had ignored all those red flags in his behaviour until it was too late and she was living in his world—if it could be described as living.

But that was then. Now she understood that to be that certain, that uncompromising, had a dark side. A dangerous side that was best avoided.

Her gaze shifted an inch to where Tiger stood watching her, the potency in his gaze undeniable. Unavoidable.

Because she couldn't avoid this man unless she let him call the police, and faced the consequences. And she couldn't do that. She couldn't fight for her brothers' freedom from behind bars.

Then again, how could she pretend to be his girlfriend?

Her arm twitched, the point of contact where his fingers had pressed against her skin tingling as if he were touching her now. If she agreed to that, then he would have to touch her, kiss her even. And she knew how he would kiss, could see his hand in her hair the better to hold her as he pressed his mouth against hers.

She took an unsteady step backwards, shivers running over her skin, her head spinning with shock and an intense, alien longing for something she didn't recognise or know how to process.

'What about your security team?' She waved her hand in the direction of Carlos. 'And your head of IT? They think I'm public enemy number one. Isn't it going to look a little bit weird if we suddenly start "dating"?'

He shrugged. 'We use white hats all the time to challenge the integrity of the security system. Obviously, it has to look real or nobody takes it seriously. If I tell them this was one of those occasions, then that's what it is. The only opinion that matters on that subject, on any subject in this building, is mine. And it's not just an opinion.' He lifted his chin and there was a dark gleam in his eyes that made her breath catch. 'It's more of a directive.'

His voice was quiet. Matter-of-fact because he wasn't bragging or bigging himself up. He didn't need to. The truth of his words was stamped into every curve and line of his gorgeous face.

Her pulse was racing. Tiger might be the most dangerous man she had ever met and yet she wasn't scared of him in the physical sense. Her fear was that he would somehow sense the heat she could feel blooming inside her.

'Even if that's true I don't see how it's going to work,' she said firmly, because she had to try, had to make him see that she would be better employed as a cyber-security asset. 'This isn't Halloween. I won't just be putting on some costume for a couple hours. You're asking me to convince people that I'm someone I'm not and I'm not an actress.'

He stared down at her, his golden gaze steady and unblinking. 'Are you saying that Abi and Hannah are in on this? That they know you've been hacking my system?'

'No, of course not.'

'Are you sure?' he persisted. 'Perhaps I should have someone bring them in and I can see what they have to say.'

She glowered at him. 'You know they haven't got a clue about any of this.'

Which, of course, meant that she had proved his point for him, she thought furiously, a fraction of a second later. The dark gleam in his eyes told her that he had been waiting for her to reach that conclusion.

Squaring her shoulders, Sydney lifted her chin. 'You're missing the point,' she said, not bothering to hide her anger and frustration. 'I wasn't acting because I *was* an assistant to Katherine.'

'True, but you were also hacking my business for personal gain.' He shook his head. 'Time's up, Ms Truitt. Make your choice.'

'It's not a choice. It's blackmail.'

His mouth twisted into a smile that made her heart thud heavily in her chest. 'No, this is retribution.'

She hated him then. Hated how he was making it seem as though he were being so reasonable when the reality was that he was bending her to his will.

'And just so we're clear, I will take silence as a refusal,' he added softly.

'This isn't legal.'

'But hacking is?' he said coolly. 'My lawyers can find a workaround. All you need to do is sign whatever I send you.' His eyes held hers as he tapped his expensive watch. 'Last chance. Yes, or no?'

'Yes,' she said through gritted teeth and the look of satisfaction on his face made her want to scream and throw things at his head.

'Good.' He sounded calm, relaxed even, as if the outcome of their conversation had never been in any doubt.

'We leave tomorrow. I've had my lawyers draw up an NDA and you'll need to sign that before you leave the building. You can wait out there. Then I'll get a car to take you home and see you to your door. Wouldn't want anything happening to you on your way home. I mean, there are so many unscrupulous people around these days,' he added, pulling his phone from his pocket.

Was that it? Sydney stared at him in confusion and a mounting anger as he began scrolling down the screen.

'You can go,' he said softly without looking at her. 'Unless you want to type out a couple of emails for old times' sake.'

She felt her cheeks grow hot. 'You know, I'm starting to think that maybe prison wouldn't be such a bad option.'

He straightened then, and held out his phone. 'Shall I make the call or would you rather do the honours?' he said in that dark way of his that made her pulse dance along her limbs. 'I guess not,' he added as she shook her head. 'In which case I think we're done here.'

There was a beat of silence.

'Not quite' she said stiffly. Ignoring the hint of shame that flared inside her, she drew a deep breath, because it had to be done. 'We haven't discussed my fee.'

Now his gaze rose to meet hers. 'Your fee?' he repeated, his mouth curving downwards in a way that thudded through her in time to her heartbeat.

The flash drive was in Tiger's possession so Harris Carver wouldn't be paying her now. Not that she was about to share that piece of information with the man in front of her. Finding out that she had a buyer and that it was Carver would be an unnecessary distraction at this point in the negotiations. What mattered was getting hold of some money, and fast. So, she was just going to have to brazen it out. There was no way around it.

'I need money,' she said flatly.

He didn't like that. Didn't like a woman asking to be paid to be his 'girlfriend'. But then it must be a first, she thought, trying to ignore the burn of his gaze. A man as beautiful and wealthy as Tiger McIntyre would have women queuing up to be invited, however briefly, into his bed.

'Tough.' His eyes were dark and dangerous then. 'Your fee is your freedom, Ms Truitt.'

Which was true but didn't make her feel any better. For a moment she contemplated appealing to his soft side and telling him the truth about her brothers. But admitting that her family were petty criminals was hardly going to help her case. And besides, Tiger was not some housecat. He didn't have a soft side.

Suddenly and fiercely, she wanted this over. Wanted to get out of this vast air-conditioned office that somehow felt small and crowded and hot because of him.

She shook her head, because she had to try. 'Right now, my freedom isn't enough.' Which hadn't always been true, she thought, with a jolt. Trapped in the house down that dirt track, miles on foot from the nearest road, body stiff from tiptoeing on eggshells, she had dreamed of freedom as a woman in a desert dreamed of finding water.

Her whole body tensed as he pushed off from the desk and took a step towards her. 'You're in no position to negotiate or make demands, Sydney, and I would advise you against thinking that is ever going to change, because it won't,' he said, and there was a husky softness to his voice that made her shiver. 'But it will vex me, which for obvious reasons I would also advise against.' His gaze narrowed on hers in a way that made her breath go shallow. 'Put simply, if you want to stay out of jail, you need to keep me sweet.'

Her lip curled. 'I thought you were on the record for not taking advantage of women,' she said tightly.

He frowned. 'I don't take advantage of women.'

Her eyes narrowed but the stupid thing was she believed him.

Yes, he was taking advantage of the situation but there was a pragmatism to his thought process that she understood. He needed a partner, a woman on his arm who could be relied upon to smile and gaze up at him adoringly and then walk away afterwards without a murmur of complaint and in a weird but logical way she fitted that remit.

Even more weirdly she had often thought how useful it would be to have a man like that to hand.

Since Noah, she had been single and celibate. She'd tried various dating apps but she was always on edge, constantly looking for the signs that she had missed with him because she couldn't trust them, or herself. Couldn't let them get close or allow things to get too deep. But there were times when it would be helpful or even just more fun to have a partner of sorts. Someone she could meet for breakfast or to take to weddings or even the occasional party. Someone who was calm and kind and intelligent, who would dance with her and laugh with her without expecting more. Someone who wouldn't try to curtail and control her when she wanted to move on.

Because she had to keep moving. Keeping one step ahead was the only way to stay safe, and it had worked just fine until today.

Feeling Tiger's gaze, she lifted her chin. 'Am I not a woman?' she said crisply.

She instantly wished she hadn't said anything because his eyes locked with hers, then moved over her face. Slowly. Then dropped again to the tiny pulse beating at the base of her throat roaming downwards over her quivering body, not missing a detail.

The atmosphere in the office was suddenly so taut that it felt as if it would shatter at any moment.

'Yes, you are,' he said slowly, and she felt her body shiver to attention, breasts suddenly and inexplicably heavy, a bud of heat pulsing between her legs.

Behind him the walls of his office seemed to be losing shape and that thing, that twitching, staticky golden thread between them that she had been pretending not to feel since walking into his office for the first time this morning, snapped taut.

Her heart was running free like a herd of wild horses.

'If there's nothing else,' she said after a moment, shifting her weight from one foot to the other like a boxer squaring up to her opponent, because that was what he was. She was clear about that. 'I'll just get my things.'

She half expected him to move but he didn't and, trying her hardest to ignore him, she reached past him for her bag, only, because she was intent on not touching him, her balance was off centre and she teetered sideways.

His hand snaked out so quickly she didn't see it move, just felt it as he caught her, her breath snatching in her throat as his arm curled around her waist, pulling her upright with such force that she found herself pinned against his warm, unyielding body.

For a moment, she couldn't process the feeling of him, the heat, the hardness. It was too much.

Except it wasn't.

Her fingers curled into his shirt. She wanted more. More heat. More hardness. More of him—

And that was a shock because she didn't like people touching her, didn't like to be touched.

Until now.

'Sydney.' The hoarseness of his voice as he said her name arrowed through her, kicking up sparks inside her so that she felt singed, and the heat of his hand was telling her things about herself she had never known, making her want things—

Her legs were softening, she was melting inside and she reached out to steady herself.

'Ouch!'

She winced. Her elbow had connected with something and a crash resounded through the cavernous office, yanking her out of her trance-like state.

What the—?

'Is everything okay in there, Mr McIntyre?' The man's voice sounded distant, as if she were dreaming it. But this wasn't a dream, she was here in Tiger's office, his chest pressing into hers, the hard shape of his thigh pushing between hers.

Only how could that be?

Tiger was her enemy, but searching inside herself she could feel nothing like loathing or disgust. Instead, her body felt taut and achy and unfulfilled because his hard, muscular chest was still temptingly within touching distance and as he moved her fingers tightened in his shirt of their own accord.

She could feel his gaze pinning her to the floor. She glanced down and saw the lamp from his desk rolling in slow, lopsided circles on the polished concrete floor. Beside it her bag lay on its side, the contents fanned out around it.

'Mr McIntyre?' The man's voice was taut and urgent now.

'Everything's fine, Carlos.' Tiger released his grip and she clutched dizzily at the desk for support. Her whole body felt hollowed out with a hunger she had never felt for any man and she could only watch dazedly as he picked up the lamp and put it back next to the pile of folders.

'I just knocked something off the desk. It's all good. In fact, Ms Truitt is just leaving, aren't you? So you can walk her to the elevator.'

Out of the corner of her eye she saw the shadowy outline of Carlos move away from the door and then her body tensed as Tiger turned towards her, because his pupils had swallowed up his irises so that his eyes were no longer gold, but black.

'Are you okay?' He stared down at her, his expression hard, glittering and unreadable, and she nodded.

She couldn't have answered Tiger's question aloud. Her

breath was gone. Her voice too. Her heart was pounding sluggishly as if she'd been drugged or hypnotised and all her blood seemed to have rushed to her cheeks and her face felt as if it were burning and yet she wanted to lean into him again and the whole thing was so confusing that she couldn't look at him any more and, ducking down, she began to pick up her things.

'Need a hand?'

'No, I don't,' she said quickly, but Tiger was already crouching beside her. His nearness made her skin feel unfamiliar, hot and tender and tingling.

'Don't,' she snapped, snatching a packet of tissues from his hand. Her voice sounded high and thin and she understood that it was revealing too much. But she couldn't do anything to change it without drawing attention to that fact and she had already given away more of herself than was sensible to this man.

There was a long silence as he stared at her for what felt like an eternity and then he spun round and walked around his desk.

'I'm sure you can find your way out. Don't forget to sign the NDA. I'll see you tomorrow morning. Make sure you're ready. If you keep me waiting, it won't be my security team knocking on your door. It'll be the NYPD.'

His eyes roamed down over her body in a way that made her feel unsteady. Unclothed.

'Dress is smart-casual but nothing flouncy or garish. Keep it subtle. Oh, and, Sydney…' He paused as she turned to face him, and now his gaze was as hot and bright and destructive as a solar flare. 'A word of warning. Any little voices in the back of your head suggesting you do a disappearing act—you would be wise to ignore them. Otherwise, you'll find out exactly what happens when you pull a tiger by the tail.'

He hadn't given her a time, she realised as she let herself into the apartment, no doubt on purpose to punish her for asking for money.

But she had no choice. She needed money and Harris Carver owed her nothing because she hadn't delivered. Her spine stiffened as she remembered their brief conversation. She hadn't told him that she'd been caught red-handed, just that she couldn't hack the McIntyre server. 'Thank you for letting me know,' he'd said and then he'd hung up.

And now she was back to square one. Worse than square one, because she had no money coming in. But at least she wasn't sitting in a police station, which was good, and in a week this would all be over, and really how bad could it be? It was just a different version of what she'd already done, only, instead of posing as an admin assistant, she would be posing as his girlfriend. So put like that, it was just more role-playing, only with a few added complications.

Her heartbeat jerked in her throat. That was one way of describing Tiger.

She felt suddenly exhausted, as if she had just finished a triathlon. As she sat down on the sofa, her phone pinged and, gazing down at the screen, she felt her breath catch in her throat. It was the NDA. She scrolled down to the bottom because otherwise it wouldn't let her sign, but she didn't bother reading it. What was the point? She was hardly going to negotiate her terms. Clicking on the screen, she signed in the box and pressed Send.

There. It was done. She wasn't going to have to face the police.

And yet she couldn't properly enjoy the feeling because now it was real. Undeniable. Unavoidable.

Her back prickled against the sofa cushions. Back in his office, it had all felt so surreal, so *unreal*. The whole time she was there she had just kept thinking, This can't be happening to me. And as she'd walked back into the apartment it had felt even more like a dream. Or a nightmare.

She glanced down at the screen, her pulse twitching.

But it was time to wake up and smell the coffee. By signing that NDA she was bound to Tiger.

Bound.

Remembering Tiger's warning about pulling a disappearing act, she got abruptly to her feet and began pacing round the apartment. Round and round as she had once paced the home that became a cage.

Could she run?

No point, she thought, a shiver running down her spine. Nobody could run for ever. Which meant she would have to find a place to hide. Only hiding was worse than running.

Her body stiffened as she remembered what it had felt like waiting to be found. Eyes closed. Braced. Breathing between clenched teeth. Waiting for the sound of his voice, his footsteps. Praying for it in the end because the silence was the most terrible thing of all.

Somewhere nearby a dog barked and her legs slowed then stopped.

No, she wasn't going to run or hide. And she didn't need to. Okay, it hadn't exactly gone according to plan, but everything was under control.

Under control? Heat rose up over her chest to scald her face as she remembered how her skin had seemed to dissolve and fuse with his in those few febrile seconds when his arm had slid around her waist and her body had pressed against his.

There had been no control, no will. She had been a creature of basic and compulsive need, impervious to the danger and absurdity of her actions.

Stalking into the kitchen area, she yanked open the refrigerator door, snatched a can of soda and pressed it against her cleavage. The last thing she had been in that moment was in control. Then again, in some ways it was good that it had happened. Now she knew what he felt like up close and if that was as bad as it got...

Only that was the problem. It hadn't been bad. On the contrary, it had been the most singularly erotic experience of her life.

Maybe, possibly, probably at some point during this sham relationship they would have to get that close again. Maybe they would even have to kiss but it would be brief, performative, but not in any way passionate. It certainly wouldn't involve tongues or open mouths because couples didn't kiss like that in public except in the movies.

And she had no intention of ever being that near to Tiger McIntyre in private again.

Staring at his laptop, Tiger frowned. That was the third time he had read that page of the document on screen and he still couldn't remember a word of it. It made no sense. He was interested in the research, respected the academics who had authored the report, but for some reason it was hard to stay focused. His mind kept drifting off.

He slammed the screen shut and shoved the laptop across the desk so hard that it collided with the lamp and he had to grab at it to stop it falling onto the floor for the second time that day.

His body tensed as a memory of the first time reared up inside his head, hazy at the edges but clear and sharp at the centre so that he could see Sydney Truitt's wide brown eyes and trembling mouth just as if she were standing there in front of him.

Although if that were the case, neither of them would be standing.

He swore under his breath. What the hell was she doing back in his head? Although it wasn't really a case of her coming back because she had never left.

His phone pinged and, glancing down at it, he felt his shoulders stiffen as he stared down at her signature. So that was that. It was official. The game was afoot.

Except it hadn't felt like a game when her body had been pressed against his. Remembering the quivering arc of her body and the way her hand had clung to him, he felt his pulse accelerate. He couldn't think of many games that involved a loss of will and purpose but, in that moment, he had forgotten why she was there and why he was there.

And it had shaken him deep down. Not just the shock of it happening, but that he hadn't wanted to let go of her.

Of course, it was understandable, he reassured himself. He had reacted without thinking and the anger and frustration and intimacy in his office had created some kind of chain reaction that had blown away his logic and willpower.

But he was back in charge now and when he held her in his arms the next time, it would be on his terms, not hers.

He pictured Sydney's face, that slight uptilt to her chin, a subtle but deliberate challenge to his authority.

In fact, this whole arrangement was going to be on his terms, as Sydney Truitt would soon find out.

CHAPTER FOUR

THAT THOUGHT WAS still front and centre in his head the following morning when he strode down the aisle of his private jet and he felt a ripple of satisfaction as he saw Sydney. She was sitting in one of the cream leather seats, that gorgeous dark red hair pulled up into one of those half-up, half-down hairstyles with a darker red ribbon, her face determinedly turned towards the window.

But she knew he was there. He could tell by the slight stiffening of her shoulders.

No doubt she was annoyed with him because he had deliberately kept her waiting for just under an hour, only rolling out of bed when Stefan, the driver he'd sent to collect Sydney, had called to let him know they had arrived at the airfield.

'Sorry, darling. I completely forgot the time,' he lied.

Now she looked up at him, slowly, reluctantly, like a prisoner of war greeting her captor, and he felt a sting of wounded pride because, yes, the alternative was being arrested but, still, he was Tiger McIntyre. Most women fell over their high heels to catch his eye but this one looked at him as if he were something that had crawled out from under a rock.

He dropped down into the seat beside her, enjoying the glint in her narrowed eyes as she moved her legs away in one seamless motion. It was a challenge he couldn't resist and he caught her hand and lifted it to his mouth, feeling immense satisfaction as he felt her surprise and then anger. Payback, he thought, for the day before. For the night he'd spent tossing restlessly in his bed thanks to the memory of her soft curves and small, stunned face intruding on his sleep.

It was a new experience for him, this incessant pulse of hunger, and one that wasn't restricted to his dreams, he realised as she angled her body away from his and his eyes followed the movement hungrily. He gritted his teeth. He had no idea why she affected him so. She was a thief and a liar and had yet to show any remorse. By rights he should despise her, and yet he couldn't remember feeling so out of control with a woman.

It was one of the reasons he'd kept her waiting. To prove that he was the one in charge of both the situation and himself. Unlike his father, he was not going to be buffeted about by his fascination for some random woman.

'I'll make it up to you,' he murmured.

'No need,' she said, smiling stiffly. 'I was perfectly happy sitting here on my own.'

'That's what I love about you. Any other woman would be bitching about having to wait but you turn it into a positive,' he said softly.

'Excuse me, Mr McIntyre, Ms Truitt.' It was Carole, one of the stewards. 'If you could put your seat belts on?'

'Of course.' Letting go of Sydney's hand, he watched

her buckle up, liking how the movement made her red hair shimmer beneath the overhead lights.

His pulse gave a jerk as the jet began to rumble down the runway. This was it. He could still stop this. And he should stop it. Sydney Truitt was bad news and trouble all tied up with a bow, metaphorically and literally.

Of their own accord, his eyes flicked to the bow on the back of her head, because all he wanted to do was tug that ribbon loose. Maybe then she would try to kiss him again as she had yesterday, he thought, watching her pale fingers tighten around the armrest as the plane lifted away from the ground.

And just like that, it was too late to do anything.

Twenty minutes later they were at cruising altitude and it was clear that any assumption that this arrangement would be happening on his terms was looking a tad premature.

Yes, Sydney smiled warmly at the stewards and answered their questions in that husky, precise way of hers that he seemed to find so fascinating, but the moment they were unobserved, she would retreat back into silence and present that profile of hers to him like a queen on a coin instead of the thief and the liar that she was.

'Are you hungry?' He didn't wait for her answer, just inclined his head slightly towards the hovering air steward. 'Good morning, Adam. I'd like three eggs, sunny side up, four rashers of bacon and an espresso to follow, and Ms Truitt will have the same. Aside from the coffee,' he added. 'She prefers an americano.'

Sydney's head jerked up and he thought she was going to say she wasn't hungry or that she didn't eat bacon or eggs, but instead she stared at him, two small lines furrowing her smooth forehead. 'How do you know how I drink my coffee?'

He shrugged. 'Intuition.'

That was a lie.

After she'd delivered his lunch and they'd had that strangely charged encounter, he had found his gaze drawn to her again and again throughout the afternoon. At one point he had wandered casually over to stand by the glass so that he could watch her return from the coffee run, her face scrunched with concentration as she made her way across the office. Even at that distance he could tell the contents of the cups from their height and colour and she had distributed the tall, skinny lattes in their cream beakers to her colleagues but kept the shorter black beaker containing an americano for herself.

'Intuition?' She stared at him suspiciously, not sure whether to believe him or not.

But why did it matter if she did or didn't? He'd never cared before what other people thought about him. With a father like his he'd had to force himself not to care, which was not easy when Gerry McIntyre was the punchline of so many jokes.

Tiger felt his jaw tighten. But he'd had the last laugh.

Taking on the name callers, calling out each and every person who thought he was as weak and dupable as his father and making it painfully and unquestionably clear to them that was not the case.

He had never looked back. But then there was no reason to do so. Everything behind him was lost or wrecked. His mother had died before he could remember her, then his grandmother had followed less than a year later. Now his father was dead too and his childhood home was a derelict shell.

All that remained was the business, and that would have gone too if he hadn't single-handedly turned it around. It hadn't been easy. On the contrary, he had earned his stripes. It was during that period of his life that he had cemented both his nickname and his reputation for ruthlessness, despatching his rivals with a speed and savagery that had left him prowling the corporate jungle almost alone so that now he was free to make the rules, not just bend them to his will.

And as the apex predator he had got used to a lot of scraping and sycophancy.

That had changed yesterday when he had generously offered this tightly wound woman sitting beside him the opportunity to be his 'girlfriend' for a week and instead of biting off his hand she had more or less told him to shove his offer where the sun didn't shine.

Such a thing had never happened before. Only, instead of hurling her to the wolves, he had doubled down, astonished and intrigued by her defiance and by the pale curve of her jaw as she'd lifted her chin to meet his gaze, because, truly, it was so alien for anyone to talk to him in that way. Which was no doubt the reason she had this effect on him.

Gauzy rays of early morning sunlight were slanting through the window onto Sydney's face and, taking that as permission to follow, he let his gaze move over her features.

She was undeniably beautiful with that red hair, dark like damp fox fur, curling over her collarbone and that matching flush of colour on those cut-glass cheekbones. The soft pink bow of her mouth was nothing short of perfection.

But instead of yesterday's office armour she was wearing black gingham capri pants, a white blouse flecked with tiny yellow flowers and low-heeled taupe-coloured sandals. His gaze steadied on her toenails, which were painted a soft, pale pink. Smart-casual, he'd said, and she was definitely erring towards the more casual end of smart-casual, but she was all the more luminous and fascinating for that.

'Have you been to Italy before?' he asked.

She shook her head.

'But you have been on a plane?' he persisted, suddenly remembering how she had clutched the armrest during take-off.

'Yes, of course. But I've never been to Europe.' She gave him a light gleam of a smile that knocked him sideways until he realised that she was smiling at Carole, who had arrived to tell them that their food was ready.

As he sat down at the table, his pulse skipped a beat as he realised that it was the first time he had eaten breakfast with a woman on his own since his grandmother died.

Like everything he did, that was a conscious decision.

He knew most people would think that dining together was the most intimate of meals and it was in the sense that fine food, low lighting and alcohol could and often did lead to sex.

But for him, sex was an end in itself. It might happen more than once. It usually did, he conceded. And then afterwards, he got up, ostensibly to shower because showering gave him a reason to get out of bed, then got dressed and left because staying over could suggest, not unreasonably, a desire to take things to the next level and he had never wanted to do that. Never wanted there to be any confusion about the kind of relationship he was offering, which was mutually satisfying but always impermanent. Sharing breakfast with a woman would simply be a humbling reminder of the mistake he'd made, the risk he'd taken. So, breakfast *à deux* was never an option.

His eyes moved to the woman beside him. But of course, Sydney was different. He *had* to eat with her so it didn't count. And anyway, it wasn't real. This was role-play with the added benefit that he was not just starring in but directing the production. This was nothing like one of his father's affairs, because there was absolutely no risk whatsoever that he would end up marrying her.

'You must have been to Vegas.' Every second person at the test plant in California seemed to have visited Sin City, either for stag or hen dos or as a consolation prize after a messy divorce.

'Vegas?' Something flickered across her face, an expression he couldn't quite place. She cleared her throat. 'Yes, I went there once.'

She glanced past his shoulder almost as if she was bored by the conversation, which was another new sensation for him. Or at least one that he couldn't remember happening since first grade.

Sydney felt everything inside her tip and roll sideways as if she were a capsizing boat. A shiver ran over her skin.

She had been to Las Vegas once, but she never allowed herself to think about it. Not because what happened in Vegas, stayed in Vegas. But because who would want to remember the place where they made the biggest mistake of their life?

It was hard to remember it now. So much time had

passed. Mostly, though, it hurt to remember the girl she'd been back then. Younger, yes, but also full of hope for a future that would be different from the kind of life all other Truitts in living memory had led. She would have a husband with a steady job. A partner with principles and a clarity of purpose.

Her fingers pressed against the smooth, pale, puckered skin on her arm. Unfortunately, his purpose had not been to cherish and honour her but to 'correct' her deficiencies. It had taken a month after their wedding before he'd had his first meltdown and thrown his plate across the kitchen because she'd put condiments on the table.

She felt Tiger's steady gaze on her face and realised that she had no idea how much time had passed since she had spoken or even if he had replied.

Fortunately, Carole returned at that moment to serve their food and she was able to legitimately turn away from him.

The rest of the flight passed surprisingly quickly. She had been slightly concerned that Tiger would want to keep on sharpening his claws on her, but, perhaps because he had eaten, he merely made a profuse and completely insincere apology and then opened his laptop and worked for the rest of the flight.

He worked hard. Harris Carver was right about that. Although that didn't absolve him of all his rule-breaking and entitlement.

Still, it was a relief not to be the focus of that dark gold gaze that saw things she needed to keep hidden. Instead, she watched a film, read some of her book and wondered after roughly every third page how his 'real' girlfriends put up with being treated in such a cavalier fashion.

Money probably. But then she was only doing this because she needed something from him too. So how was she different from them?

Nibbling her thumbnail, she listed off all the ways she could think of. Firstly, there was no actual relationship. No trust. No history. No hopes. They didn't even like each other and obviously there was no intimacy.

Her pulse stalled, her memory rewinding like a car spinning on black ice to that moment in his office when she'd almost kissed him.

She hadn't forgotten it. She had tried to, of course, but it seemed to have burned itself into her brain. Thankfully, it was probably a common enough occurrence for Tiger to have dismissed it from his mind but, glancing up, she felt a different shiver scamper through her body. Instead of looking at the laptop screen, he was staring at her in that intent way of his, his pupils flickering. Was he remembering it too?

It didn't matter one way or the other, she told herself firmly.

She couldn't change the past. She knew that better than anyone. But you could choose how to live your life, make decisions about which risks were worth taking and which would be avoided, and kissing Tiger fell unequivocally in the second category.

An hour later, the jet landed with barely a shudder on the runway at the private airfield on the Italian mainland.

There was a car waiting for them on the runway and she knew there was a bridge across the lagoon so she had assumed that they would drive into the city but, after twenty minutes, the driver turned off the main road and she saw the shimmer of water.

'What's happening?'

Tiger glanced over at her. 'We're swapping onto a boat.'

As explanations went it was minimal but there was no time to question him further. The car had already come to a stop, and now the driver was opening the door. It was a short walk to a covered jetty and then Tiger was helping her into a glossy, wooden speedboat.

He sat down beside her, letting his leg graze against hers in a way that was without doubt deliberate, but she was tired now. It had been a long day and the air was cool and his thigh was warm so she could reasonably allow herself to stay where she was. Leaning back against the plush leather upholstery, she watched eagerly for her first glimpse of Venice.

All she knew about the city was from the movies and it felt odd seeing a place so familiar for the first time rising out of the water. But even at night and at a distance it was mesmerisingly beautiful.

'Come si sente suo cugino, Angelo? Ben preparato, spero?'

She blinked as Tiger leaned forward and began speaking fast, fluent Italian to the driver. He caught sight of her expression, and his mouth curved up at one corner.

'His cousin is taking part in the *gondolino* race this year. I was just asking him if he was feeling ready.'

Tiger talking to the driver of the boat in Italian was distracting enough but when that was combined with the way his hair was being blown in the wind and the glint in his eyes, it was a moment before she realised that the city was fading into the distance.

Her heart thudded against her ribs. 'What's happening? Is there a problem?'

Dropping back down onto the seat beside her, he shook his head. 'No problem.'

'But surely the hotel is that way.'

'What hotel?'

She blinked. 'The hotel we're staying at.'

'We're not staying in a hotel. I don't like the crowds and, besides, I have a villa here.' His mouth did that curving thing again and she felt it thump through her in time to her heart as he corrected himself. 'Not here in the city. It's on one of the other islands in the lagoon.'

Sydney stared at him, her head spinning. She had assumed, wrongly it turned out, that they would be staying in a hotel surrounded by staff and other guests. But that wasn't the case because he had a villa.

Of course he did.

And there was not much point in worrying about it now, she thought as the speedboat accelerated. Finally, the driver shouted something over his shoulder and the boat slowed to a crawl. Her heart gave a thump as Tiger turned towards her and said softly, 'Just remember, you're my girlfriend and you're madly in love with me.'

There was no right response to that statement, or none that she could think of, but she didn't need to, because they were pulling up alongside a wooden jetty that lit up as they got closer. A young man wearing smart shorts and a black polo shirt stepped forward to pick up their cases.

'*Bentornato, Signor McIntyre, e benvenuti, Signorina Truitt.* I hope you had a pleasant journey.'

Tiger took her hand again to help her off the boat and this time he didn't let go, but she was expecting that. It was incredibly quiet after the thump of the boat, but it was quieter even than that. Almost as if this were a desert island, not a playground for wealthy tourists.

They were walking so swiftly that she had only the briefest glimpse of the villa—large, three storeys, with lots of arched windows—and then they were inside and a middle-aged woman with sleek dark hair stepped forward to greet them.

'This is Silvana. She doesn't speak much English. Most of the staff don't. It means I have to practise my Italian.'

'What about the other tourists? Are they just Italian?'

'There are no other tourists. This is my island.'

Of course it was.

He was walking as he talked and she let him lead her upstairs. 'You can have the guided tour tomorrow, but this is our room,' he added, so casually that it took a moment for the implication of his words to hit home.

And then everything lurched inside her.

Sydney's eyes narrowed and Tiger felt the air sharpen between them.

'Our room?' She frowned.

'Yes, darling. Our room,' he repeated. Yet another thing he had never had to do before. He sensed rather than saw Silvana turn. Moments later he heard the door click shut.

'What the hell do you think you're playing at?' Sydney snapped, her soft mouth curving into a snarl that revealed small white even teeth. She tugged her hand free, her body rigid with fury and outrage.

'I could ask you the same thing,' he said mildly, and with what was an admirable amount of restraint given that they were alone and he knew exactly what it felt like to feel her body against his.

'Meaning?' Her hands curled into fists by her sides.

'You're supposed to be my girlfriend, remember?'

'Only in public.' She waved her hand wildly to encompass all four corners of the room. 'We're not in public here.'

'You and I have a deal,' he said, adopting a soothing tone that was designed to do the opposite of soothe. Because, frankly, why was he having to explain himself? Again? 'I gave you a choice and the choice you made was obviously going to include us sharing a room. Surely you understood that?'

Her hands clenched and unclenched by her sides.

'Why obviously? We've only just started seeing one another. Maybe I have strict parents so I've insisted on separate rooms?'

Separate rooms? For a moment he was stunned by her suggestion. It had literally never happened before, and in this instance, it couldn't.

The reason she was here, the *only* reason in fact, was so that he would have a partner. Having a beautiful woman on his arm was part of his brand. Like the watch he wore and the handmade suits and even his nickname. It was his armour. All of it was designed to intimidate, to discourage people from getting too close, because everyone had their own agenda, particularly women.

He switched his gaze to Sydney's face. 'And what exactly do you imagine everyone is going to think about that?'

'Exactly what you tell them to think, I expect,' she said, and he felt the huskiness in her voice pulse in all the wrong places. 'After all, the only opinion that matters on that subject, on any subject, is yours. And it's not just an opinion, is it, Mr McIntyre?' She lifted his chin. 'It's more of a directive.'

He laughed then. Partly to cover up his astonishment at being bested by her because, damn, she was smart, and she was right too, even though it pained him to admit it. And partly, and this was even more astonishing, because he was enjoying himself.

In the space of forty-eight hours she had ignored and interrupted him, defied and challenged him and now she was making him laugh.

He couldn't remember the last time a woman had done that.

Not because he didn't find things amusing. Despite what most people thought, he had a sense of humour, but laughing meant you were relaxed, and being relaxed would require him on some level to let down his guard and he had never done that with any woman because there was a risk that he might turn into his father if he did so.

But Sydney was different. This 'relationship' was different. He didn't have to worry about things getting out of hand or being misinterpreted. They had a deal, and so he could relax.

Which must be why this felt more real than any of the so-called relationships he'd had in the past.

And maybe him laughing like that caught her off guard

or perhaps it was just the sudden break in the tension between them, but her mouth was pulling at the corner and he was suddenly desperate to see the smile that was trying to break free.

'That's how it works,' he agreed, and he had that same sudden intense need to touch her just as he'd had back in his office. He reached out to touch her face—

Her eyes snapped wide open, and she took an unsteady step back, and for a moment she just stared at him in the taut silence that filled the room.

'Unless,' she said at last, her voice a light taunt, 'you were simply bragging. Or projecting. Is that why you suggested this charade? Because you're not the man you pretend to be?'

He wasn't enjoying himself now. Her words had hit home.

Which was ironic, as he hadn't had a home since he was four years old when his grandmother had died and he'd moved back to live with his father. From then he had felt like a guest, and often not a welcome one. His heart thumped against his ribs. But Gerry had been oblivious because Gerry had recently fallen in love again. So Tiger had decided that he wanted no part of love. That love was blind, and it was dangerous.

But now this woman, this thief, this imposter, had got past his carefully constructed walls. And he had let her, invited her in no less. He felt a rush of fury with himself, but mostly with Sydney for turning him into a stranger. For making him feel like the kind of stupid, susceptible man he'd sworn never to become.

'You're getting confused, *Sierra*,' he said coolly. 'You

see, I'm perfectly clear about who I am. But maybe I didn't make it clear enough to you, so let me rectify that right now.'

Reaching into his trouser pocket, he pulled out the flash drive and held it up between his fingers.

'I am the man standing between you and a long prison sentence. So if I say jump, you jump. Real high. And you keep on jumping until I say stop.'

Silence.

'Do you like threatening people?' she said finally.

No, he thought, his chest pinching as he stared down at her. She looked as though she was bracing herself just as she had in his office and he didn't like how that made him feel. Didn't like that he was making her feel that way.

It didn't help that those clothes made her look younger than she had yesterday. He might even have said vulnerable, if her chin hadn't tilted up pugnaciously.

It was enough to make him come to his senses.

'Do you like stealing?' he countered, severe suddenly, although he was far more distracted by the flags of colour on her cheeks than was sensible.

Another silence.

Damn it. He glanced round the bedroom, his spine taut with frustration. This was not what he had imagined. Then again, he hadn't actually given much thought to how it would work in reality, just signed off on the concept.

'I'm not sure what you were expecting to happen.'

'Don't do that.' Her voice was hoarse when she answered and her eyes shimmered with a heat that he wanted to immerse himself in. 'Don't try to make me out to be the problem here. This was your idea. You're not going to make me responsible for your lack of forward planning.'

He stared at her, his teeth on edge. It wasn't lack of forward planning that had brought them to this moment, but arrogance and past experience. To put it another way, he couldn't remember the last time a woman had not wanted to share his bed because there had never been one.

'Look, the bed is big enough that we don't have to interact.'

His body tensed painfully as his brain began to offer up a slideshow of several possible permutations of what interacting with Sydney might look like.

'It's not just the size of the bed. It's the fact that you'll be in it. There isn't going to be an "interaction" of that sort between us.' Wide brown eyes accompanied that dismissive statement, but the sudden splashes of high colour on her cheeks told a different story and he remembered that shimmering, explosive moment they'd shared in his office back in New York.

She was stubborn, almost as stubborn as he was. She was also out of her depth and she didn't have his stamina for fighting her corner. More importantly, he could see her pulse hammering against the pale skin on her throat and that glitter in her eyes.

'Nothing is going to happen. Unless you want it to,' he added, because he could still remember her soft, stunned gaze and the way her fingers had splayed against his arm. And he was also arrogant enough to assume that she would be no different from any other women in his life.

Her pupils flared. 'Then I hope you enjoy waiting because I will never want you.'

Wrong, he thought, and he wanted to prove that, to yank her against him and finish what had started in his office. Instead, he took a step closer, close enough that he could see her pulse fluttering down her throat.

'And I hope you enjoy sleeping on the right side of the bed, but if you don't, then I'm afraid you'll have to choose between the floor, the couch or the bathtub because while you're here with me, this is your bedroom, and this subject is now closed.'

She stared up at him in silence, and he felt a tick of irritation.

'Right, I suggest we go and get something to eat.' What now? He broke off, frowning as she shook her head.

'I don't want anything to eat. I'm tired. I want to go to sleep.'

'You can't go to sleep,' he said impatiently. 'It's only four p.m. in New York. Plus, you've missed a meal.'

'I don't care.' There was strain in her voice now but with that same storm in her eyes as before. 'I want to go to sleep.'

'Fine. Have it your way. Just don't blame me when you wake up and can't get back to sleep, because that's what will happen. And when it does, I suggest you think long and hard about how you're going to make this arrangement between us work. Unless, of course, you'd prefer to take your chances with the police, which, frankly, I wouldn't recommend, but given you seem determined to do the opposite of whatever I suggest, knock yourself out.'

Sydney held her breath as Tiger spun round and stalked past her, and the walls shuddered as he slammed the door behind him, and then it was over. He was gone.

She was alone.

She was shaking inside. Not from fear any more, although it was not fear of him but of the idea of sharing a bed with a stranger. Now, though, she felt frustrated. He was impossible. Unreasonable. Thoughtless. And she was stupid for thinking this could ever work.

And for not thinking about the possible sleeping arrangements for their week together. How had she not thought about that?

Mainly because back in New York, and even on the way over to the island, she had been trying so hard to believe that none of this was happening that she hadn't allowed herself to think that far. Her eyes fixed on the bed. Because if she'd thought about 'this' she would never have been able to do what was needed.

As she stared at the bed, her mouth felt suddenly dry. It was a very big bed but the idea of sharing it with Tiger made her heart thud painfully hard inside her chest. What did he wear in bed? And what if they moved while they were sleeping and ended up touching?

That moment in his office reared up inside her, shimmering bright and tactile, and she was flushed with the heat of it, skin tingling, breasts aching and heavy. No, she thought, her pulse scrambling for a footing. That wasn't real. Whatever she had felt then was just a combination of gravity and panic and proximity.

Wasn't it?

And then, quite suddenly, she felt tired, the have-to-sit-down-before-I-fall-down kind of tired that made thinking impossible. She needed to sleep, and now, and, walking over to the bed, she pulled back the cover and climbed in, her eyes closing like shutters as her brain powered down to silence.

Tiger had been right, Sydney thought four hours later as she woke in the darkness and stared blearily at the time on her phone screen. It was three a.m.

Three a.m. here but nine p.m. in New York, which was no doubt why she had never felt more wide awake. Or hungrier.

Except that wasn't true. There had been frequent days with Noah when food had been a privilege, not a right.

But Noah wasn't here. Nor was Tiger. She had known that maybe even before her eyes had snapped open. Which must mean he had decided to sleep in another room. She felt what must be relief only it felt oddly almost like disappointment. Or hunger, she told herself firmly as her stomach rumbled loudly. She reached over to switch on the bedside lamp and she sat up, blinking into the light.

Why was she so hungry? They had eaten lunch and had cakes and coffee in the afternoon, but not enough, apparently.

Maybe a glass of water might help. Her throat tightened because she didn't want to do that. Having a glass of water would mean accepting that food was not an option. It would mean that Noah was still inside her head, controlling her, crushing her, and that wasn't an option either.

She wasn't some cowed prisoner; she was Tiger McIntyre's girlfriend. Or at least that was what everyone believed.

Heart pounding, she threw back the covers and realised she was still fully clothed. Her bags had been unpacked and the contents neatly placed in the walk-in wardrobe. Ignoring the beautiful shirts hanging from the rail, she found the T-shirt she wore to sleep in, stripped, then pulled it over her head.

Back in the bedroom, she picked up the luxurious, quilted bathrobe that was artistically draped over a beautiful linen-covered armchair. It felt glorious, she thought as she wrapped the belt tightly around her waist, soft and thick but light, like being enveloped in a cloud.

The next step was to go downstairs and, not giving herself time to think, she stalked across the room and opened the door. There was nobody there. Obviously, because it was three o'clock in the morning, but there were table lamps lit and she made her way downstairs.

Having not had the 'tour', she had no idea where the kitchen was, but it was the first room she found, which seemed like a good sign. There was no sign of a fridge, but then a house this big would surely have a larder.

It did.

Sydney stared around the regimented rows of condiments and snacks and jars of pasta and flour and grains. Her stomach rumbled appreciatively. It was an Aladdin's cave of food, teeming with every possible ingredient and treat.

And there was a cavernous fridge. Tentatively, she pulled on the handle. Oh, goodness, it had a door within a door so that you could see inside without opening it. She licked her lips as her eyes snagged on a plate of salad with tomatoes and bread and olives.

This would be perfect, she thought, opening the second door to retrieve the dish, then shutting the fridge doors and turning—

She gasped and almost dropped the plate.

Tiger was standing there, laptop in hand, his body blocking the doorway to the larder. 'You know, this is becoming a habit with you. First you try to steal my IP, now you're taking my panzanella.'

CHAPTER FIVE

SYDNEY BLINKED.

Her heart was beating so loudly she was surprised that Tiger couldn't hear it. If only she had stayed upstairs. It was the latest in an ongoing, ever-growing list of regrets she had about the last few days. But there was nothing she could do about that now.

She cleared her throat. 'Is that what this is called?'

Tiger nodded, and then he walked towards her and every single cell in her body exploded with panic, except it wasn't panic. She knew panic all too well, and this was more complicated.

And contradictory.

'It's a Tuscan bread salad. I have my chef make it every time I visit.'

'Here, you have it.' She held it out towards him, and then wished she hadn't as the movement made the robe part around her throat and she felt the flick of his gaze lick her skin like a flame.

'Or,' he said after several beats of silence, 'we could share it.'

They ate in the kitchen. Tiger didn't bother to decant the salad onto a second plate so it was a case of sharing.

'My bad—' Her pulse twitched as his fork collided with hers as they both tried to spear the same piece of tomato at the same time.

'You have it,' she said quickly, fingers tightening around the handle of the fork. She couldn't remember the last time she had shared a plate of food with anyone and it felt oddly intimate. Too intimate. It was the kind of thing a new couple might do on their first date, order a dessert and then smugly ask the waiter for two spoons.

But she and Tiger were not a couple and, even though superficially this had all the component parts of one, this definitely wasn't a date. More it was a ceasefire.

'You're the guest,' he countered.

Her eyes flicked to his face. 'I thought I was a pain.'

In the low lighting of the kitchen, his hair and eyes were dark, only his skin looked golden. 'Oh, you're that too.'

She had been here before with a different man who had made it his mission to point out her flaws. But this didn't feel like that at all. Absurdly it felt as if his words were meant as a compliment.

'I mean, it's kind of what you do, isn't it? Being two things at once.'

That wasn't a compliment but his voice lacked the sting it would have if he were digging at her and the slight uptilt to his mouth made her want to lean closer and trace the curve of his lips—

Shying away from the ridiculousness of that thought, she let her gaze drop to the plate, staring down admiringly at the olive-oil-strewn chunks of bread and glossy tomatoes, as if that, not him and his all too fascinating face, was the most important thing in the room just then.

'But I was being a bit of a pain too,' he said softly.

Glancing up, she found him watching her in that incisive way of his.

'A bit?' She raised an eyebrow.

Tiger leaned back in his seat, his strong fingers stroking the rim of his water glass, and she suddenly wished that it were New York time here so that Silvana or some other member of staff would be bringing them food just as they had on the plane, and there would be something to distract her from this intense and intensely beautiful man sitting opposite her.

'Okay, I was a pain earlier. I hadn't thought through some of the hands-on practicalities of our arrangement.'

Hands-on. Remembering the seeking press of his fingers as he had pulled her against him, she felt her face get warm.

'I didn't think about it either,' she said quickly.

He tilted his chin back. 'True, but as you so rightly said, this was my idea.'

It was more of an acknowledgement than an apology but that in itself felt seismic. During her brief, exhausting and terrifying marriage, she had always been wrong and it had taken years to shift that thinking.

'And I should have realised that you might not be comfortable sharing a bed.' She must have tensed because she felt his eyes flick to her face.

'So, I was thinking maybe you might be happier in another room.'

Now her eyes flicked to his. She hadn't expected that and something of her surprise must have shown on her face because he frowned. 'I know I haven't offered you much in the way of evidence but I'm not a monster, Sydney.'

'I don't think you're a monster,' she said quietly. 'And I get why it makes sense for us to sleep in the same room.'

His eyes were steady and precise on her face. 'I can take the sofa.'

'Or you could share the bed.' Her voice sounded different, and now his gaze enveloped her, holding her captive with hypnotic intensity.

'Like you said, it's big enough.'

'It is.' His voice was different now too. 'But only if you're okay with that.'

She nodded. 'I am.' She was. And she knew that shouldn't make sense, and yet it did. Because of him.

Maybe he hadn't formally apologised but Tiger had admitted to going too far; what was more, he was trying to make amends for how he'd acted.

Only this wasn't just about him, it was about her too. About how, even though she was divorced, she hadn't put her relationship with Noah behind her. For so long now, she had been too scared to let anyone get close but, probably because none of this was real, she felt safe enough with Tiger to do so. Not just physically, but emotionally.

After all, she was playing a role. Her actual feelings weren't involved.

And a part of her did miss being intimate, being held, being close to someone, which was completely understandable. Although it was surprising that it should be Tiger who had made her finally admit that to herself. To cover her confusion she said quickly, 'But thank you for giving me the choice.'

'So, you believe me now?' He was watching her with a

narrow sort of gaze as if he cared about her answer. 'That I'm not a monster?'

'You're not a monster. I mean, you like getting your own way.'

'You sound like my housekeeper.'

That smile.

She felt her stomach lurch, only this time it had nothing to do with hunger and her heart thudded hard as heat surged through her. A dizzying, dangerous heat that she felt everywhere, almost as if those callused hands were touching her, caressing her—

'What do you mean?' She didn't really care. It was just something to say to clear her head but as his eyes met hers, she was suddenly curious.

A knot formed lower down in her belly as he shifted back in his seat and the crooked smile curving his mouth deepened a fraction at the corners. 'When I came downstairs, she guessed we'd had a row about where you were sleeping. I think it's fair to say that she was surprised, but also pleased. She thinks I have things too easy. With women. She thinks it's bad for me.' His smile twisted. 'She doesn't say so to my face, but she has a way of conveying her opinion with an eyebrow or the slightest of shrugs.'

'And do you? Have things too easy? With women?' she blurted out before her brain could apply the brakes.

Her whole body tensed, the reaction both a learned response and a survival instinct hardwired in her DNA to the sudden tautness in the air that followed her question.

Tiger shifted in his seat.

'I like women. And they like me,' he said, putting down

his fork. 'Or they think they do until they realise that I'm not in it for the long haul.'

'And that's a problem, is it? The long haul?'

He nodded. 'I think relationships are best kept simple.'

She agreed. Simple was good but safe was better. Not that she was interested in relationships. For any relationship to work there had to be trust and outside her family she didn't trust anyone. And yet she was having this surprisingly frank conversation with Tiger.

'By simple, I'm guessing you mean that you just want sex?'

He laughed. 'That's maybe putting it a little too simply. But yes, I suppose in an ideal world, I think it would be easier for most people if they accepted that sex was all they wanted a lot of the time. Only humans seem determined to make things more complicated, so we have marriage and romance and love.'

Been there, done that, she thought bleakly, and once was enough. And for her it had not been complicated at all.

Marriage was a cage; romance was a hoax. As for love?

Love was the most dangerous of them all. So much more dangerous than you were told. It was a promise that got broken every single day.

'I'm not interested in any of that.' He pushed the empty plate away from him as if to underscore that sentiment.

'I'm not interested in any of that either.' She hesitated for a moment then, putting her fork down, she said quietly, 'What does interest you, then?'

Her heart slowed to a crawl as silence stretched between them.

'Work. Building my business. And the moon. Ever since

I was a kid, I wanted to go there—' He glanced past her
to the dark square of sky outside. 'It always felt like it was
watching me, seeing me.'

It seemed like an odd thing to say. She couldn't imagine
a situation where Tiger wasn't seen.

'I suppose it would be quiet.'

He nodded and there was another long, shifting silence
and then abruptly he leaned forward, his eyes suddenly
very golden. 'So, was it the truth?'

She stared at him, confused, not just by his question,
which made no sense at all, but by the way he was looking at her so closely as if she was a puzzle he was trying
to figure out. 'Was what the truth?'

'What you said about your family being strict. Are they?'

No, she thought. Her childhood home had not quite been
lawless, but there had been very few rules. And she had
hated it, because every morning when she'd woken, anything could have happened. Maybe that was why she was so
good at hacking. She accepted the impossible, the random,
the topsy-turvy and she had learned to let it flow round her
while she restored order.

But she could imagine how that would sound to Tiger,
how he would react. She had heard it so many times already, some version of the 'apple doesn't fall far from the
tree'. She didn't need to hear him say it too.

'They're not strict,' she said slowly. 'But they have lines
they won't cross.'

Her family might turn a blind eye to selling car parts that
might be stolen. But they weren't violent or controlling or
abusive. For example, they wouldn't bang someone's face

against a steering wheel because they had missed a spot of
dirt on the windscreen.

The memory had crept in uninvited, but she couldn't
look away. One tiny little tooth, white like a pearl, and
blood, red, slick, gleaming in the Nevada sunlight. So much
blood.

She shoved the memory back forcefully into the margins
because obviously she wasn't going to tell Tiger any of that.

Or could she?

The question shocked her almost out of her skin. She was
definitely suffering jet lag, she told herself, if she thought
that was an option. It was the only possible explanation for
why she was considering something that made absolutely
no sense whatsoever.

She had never told anyone about Noah, not even the
police.

And she especially couldn't tell Tiger. He wasn't her
confidant.

He wasn't even her friend.

He was the man who had offered her a way out of the
fire into the frying pan. And he would walk her straight
back into the fire without a qualm because nobody got as
rich as Croesus by being soft and *simpatico*. It didn't matter that he had sat and shared a salad with her or that she
had momentarily imagined feeling safe with him.

If she told him about Noah, then he would ask questions
and any answers she gave would raise more questions. Only
how could she answer those questions? To do so would
mean revealing more than she was willing to share and she
didn't want to think about the person she had been back

then. Didn't want to show weakness when it felt as though they had reached some kind of equality.

'What about your family? Are they strict?'

For a fraction of a second, she thought he wasn't going to reply but then he did another of those infinitesimal shrugs.

'I have no family.'

He glanced at the expensive watch on his wrist. 'You should probably be able to sleep now.'

It was a dismissal, just as if they were back in the office. Except she was wearing a bathrobe.

'Is there a dishwasher?' She stood up, reaching for the plate—

'You don't need to.'

He moved at the same time, his chair scraping against the floor as he got to his feet, his hand covering hers.

Move, she told herself. But she couldn't. It was as if the touch of his hand had stopped time. Stopped everything. There was nothing but the silence and the darkness and the heat of his skin and his nearness as the air grew thicker.

For a second they both stared at each other. Every single nerve ending in her body was flickering like a malfunctioning circuit board.

Only she didn't feel broken.

She felt whole and right and sure, and she stepped forward and clasped his head between her hands and fitted her mouth against his.

And everything just stopped.

She felt a jolt of shock as if she hadn't decided to kiss him. But then in a way she hadn't. It had been more of an imperative, a challenge to be met, a need to be satisfied. Curiosity and desire in their most primitive and basic form.

She couldn't remember any kiss feeling like this. It was a wildfire tearing through the darkened outback, torching everything in its path. A wall of flame that altered everything it touched. It was possessive and intoxicating. Devastating and reckless and so necessary.

And that was shocking in a different way. That she should want his mouth on hers. That there was no terror pulling her under at his closeness.

For the first time in six years, she wanted this, wanted him.

He was pulling her towards him now, his hand fumbling clumsily at her waist, anchoring her body against his so that she could feel the hard press of his chest and thighs.

The lights beneath the kitchen units spun and blurred behind them, bright and fast like a carousel, but the real world, the world of lawyers and contracts and threats and failure, was so far away.

There was only him.

Tiger.

Here. With his free hand sliding upwards through her hair in one smooth motion, fingers warm and strong, his mouth rough and tender. He parted her lips and deepened the kiss and the fierceness of him took her breath away and she heard herself moan. Then he was lifting her against him and her few remaining thoughts grew gauzy, weightless, unimportant.

Somewhere in the house a clock chimed loudly and she jerked backwards and her heart, which had stopped beating when he had touched her, started up again at twice the pace.

'If you've changed your mind about where you want me

to sleep—' He sounded as shell-shocked as she felt. Nervous almost, although she must be imagining that.

She cleared her throat. 'I haven't,' she said quickly.

'Okay, then.' He was back in control. 'Like you said, the bed is big enough.' He glanced at his watch. 'Why don't you go on up? You don't need to wait for me,' he added. 'I have some work to finish up.'

His dark gold gaze held her captive momentarily and then he turned to pick up the plate and she didn't quite run but she moved swiftly through the silent house and back into the bedroom. Undoing the robe, she let it drop to the floor and climbed into bed, her body shimmering and strange to her, and she stayed that way when he slid in beside her as the light began to creep beneath the shutters.

'Dovrei preparare una caffettiera fresca, Signor McIntyre? Questo è freddo.'

Glancing up at his housekeeper, Tiger shook his head. 'No, *grazie*, Silvana.'

Normally he could drink any amount of coffee without any noticeable side effects at all, but today he had barely drunk more than a quarter of the French press that Silvana had brought to the table and he was already suffering from a sensory overload.

Or maybe the cause of his twitching pulse and headache was not the contents of the coffee press but the contents of the yellow shirtdress sitting opposite him in the soft Venetian sunlight.

He had woken early, but when he'd rolled over, the bed had been empty and the sheet smoothed flat as if she had never been there. As if he had dreamt her.

But she wasn't a figment of his imagination, any more than that kiss.

Yet here she was sitting opposite him, calmly sipping her coffee as if nothing had happened in the kitchen. And he didn't know whether to be relieved or angry. When he'd strolled onto the terrace, he hadn't expected her to smile but her mouth had curved up at the corners because Silvana was there too, he'd realised a moment later. But then she'd tilted her head up so that he'd caught a glimpse of the smooth arc of her throat and he'd leaned in and brushed his lips against hers.

She had stiffened fractionally and then her lips had parted and he'd had to fight against every urge to deepen the kiss because this arrangement was on his terms and that meant being able to pull back.

'Buongiorno,' he'd said softly, lifting his mouth and pulling out a chair in one smooth moment as Silvana had returned with a bowl of freshly baked *cornettos*. Sydney had selected an almond-flavoured one and as he watched her pull it apart, he wondered why the process of sharing breakfast with her today seemed so much less of a big deal than it had done on the plane.

No doubt it was because they had already eaten off the same plate last night or the early hours of this morning, depending on which time zone you applied. Although, right now, nothing seemed to matter as much as getting her to keep looking up at him like that so that he could see the pale underside of her neck.

He leaned forward casually. 'Did you sleep well?'

She nodded. '*Ho dormito come un ghiro*. Like a dormouse?'

He raised an eyebrow. It was an Italian phrase, but Sydney didn't speak Italian. 'Where did you pick that up?'

'I did some miming to Silvana.' She pressed the palms of her hands together and rested her head on them. 'She told me what to say in Italian and then I checked on my phone to make sure I hadn't got the wrong end of the stick.'

'Or mistaken fireflies for lanterns. *Prendere lucciole per lanterne.* It's the closest to getting the wrong end of the stick in Italian.'

He leaned a little closer, drawn to the flicker of curiosity in her brown eyes because, other than himself, he couldn't think of a single person he knew who would be interested in learning idiomatic Italian for a week-long trip.

'So, you like languages? I thought hackers were all maths nerds.'

Her eyes narrowed. 'Do I look like a nerd to you?'

No, he thought. She didn't. In that dress, with that hair and those toenails, she looked as if she were about to sashay down the Rio Terà de le Carampane to meet some girlfriends for lunch at Terrazza Cattana.

She shrugged. 'Coding is like a language. Equations are just sentences with numbers. At school I never really understood that. I thought words weren't my thing. Reading, writing was always such a struggle, so my teachers told me to focus on maths.' She glanced away as if she was remembering a classroom somewhere and he found himself trying to picture her as a child. Skinny, he thought. Plaits and maybe a brace, he thought, remembering the way she had covered her mouth sometimes.

'What changed?'

Her shoulders stiffened. It was the smallest of movements, so subtle that another man might not have noticed it. But thanks to his father, he was an expert at reading people and there was something about that infinitesimal shift that made his chest tighten.

'I realised that letting other people set your boundaries was the easy option. Pushing back feels harder at the time. And it feels like an unnecessary risk to take, because you might fail.' There was an odd undertone to her voice that pulled at something inside him. She was choosing her words with care, he realised, not just because she wanted to be clear about what she was trying to say. She was also trying to conceal some things too.

'But if you don't push back, you stop being you. And then every day a little piece of you will disappear until finally there's nothing left.'

Sydney felt her stomach tighten. Tiger was lounging back in his chair, his face bathed in sunlight, one arm resting lightly along the back of the chair beside him, his long legs stretching out casually beneath the table. He was wearing a pale blue, short-sleeved linen shirt and loose cream-coloured trousers and he looked every inch the relaxing business mogul on vacation.

Except his eyes. Which were staring at her intently.

'That's quite a theory,' he said at last.

She forced herself to shrug but inside her head was spinning. It was true, she did feel that way, but she had never articulated it out loud because it wasn't just reading and writing she found hard. Speaking her mind, making herself heard, was also a problem. It was another reason why she liked working with computers. Coding didn't require actual speech.

But there was something about this man that made her eloquent.

No, not this man, she corrected herself quickly. It was the situation. Being here, in Italy, on this island. It felt as though she were outside space and time, outside herself.

'In my job, there's a lot of sitting around waiting for things to reveal themselves so I get a lot of time to think.'

Or she could just say the first, stupid thing that came into her head.

Her words reverberated loudly around the terrace and her jaw clenched tight as Tiger's eyes flicked to her face.

'Am I to assume by job you mean the part in the day when you hack my server in order to steal my IP? Rather than what I was paying you to do?' Tiger said softly. He hadn't moved a muscle but the air around them seemed to shudder a little and she swore silently because they had come full circle. The guarded rapprochement of moments earlier had evaporated and Tiger was once again the man who had stared down at her in his office with such contempt.

'I was just trying to—' she began, but he cut her off.

'No matter. You're here to do a different job now and time is moving on.' His gaze sharpened. 'I'll give you a quick tour of the house and then we need to go over a few things, get our stories straight.'

The villa was beautiful and she would have liked to stop and admire the gilt and the marble and the tapestries and the glittering chandeliers, but the tour was brief and perfunctory, with Tiger opening doors and listing off rooms at breakneck speed so that she had little more than a blurred impression of pink and dark red and burnished gold.

Finally, they made their way upstairs and he ticked off the various bedrooms and bathrooms until they reached their bedroom, where the housekeeper stood waiting by the door.

'Ah, Silvana, *è tutto pronto*?'

The housekeeper nodded. *'Quasi.'*

'Bene.' He turned back to Sydney, gesturing through the door. 'Shall we?'

She stepped into the bedroom and stopped. There was a rail in the middle of the room and hanging from the rail were clothes. Not her clothes, but fluid, figure-hugging couture that came without price tags because only people who didn't care about money would buy them.

'What are these?' She turned towards Tiger, who frowned, unsurprisingly, because it was obvious what they were.

'They're for you to wear this week. It's not just the regatta and the ball, there are other events and you need to look the part. You're welcome,' he added, his mouth twisting, clearly underwhelmed by what he perceived as a lack of gratitude on her part.

'What's wrong with my clothes?' she said, pushing back against the memories of Noah throwing her favourite jeans in the trash. As on everything else, her ex-husband had had opinions on what she should wear. And now Tiger seemed to think he could have an opinion too. Only it was more than that. Ever since she'd talked about her job at breakfast, his mood had shifted. But why was he so angry about something he already knew? It made no sense, only that was the worst kind of anger to manage.

'I knew I was going to have to borrow something for the ball, because I don't have a ball gown, but—'

'Are you being serious?' he said after a moment, his tone cool and sardonic. 'What you're wearing is fine for here, but you need something more high-end.' He flicked the sleeve of a beautiful dark green dress.

'You said smart-casual.'

His golden gaze seemed to tear into her. 'I meant for the flight. Obviously, I'm not expecting you to wear your own clothes when we're in public.'

Sydney stared at the contents of the rail, a small shiver winding through her body. 'Why "obviously"? My back-story is that I'm someone you met through work. We're not pretending that I come from money.'

'Because that's how this works.' He was impatient now. 'Because I'm not just a guest, I'm a sponsor of the race and the ball and you're going to attend those events as *my* girl-friend, which means you have to wear the kind of clothes that a girlfriend of mine would wear. Most women would be happy, grateful, excited.'

Trying to stay calm and centred, Sydney let her gaze move over the shimmering silks and gauzy wisps of chif-fon. 'But I wouldn't wear anything like this. It's not who I am.'

'You are who I say you are.'

His voice was harsh but it was the shrug accompany-ing that blunt statement that made the floor ripple beneath her feet as if it were made of quicksand, because that tiny, careless shift of his shoulders was more than just proof that he was unmoved by, and impervious to, her point of view, her wishes, her feelings.

It was a sharp, stomach-churning reminder of how quickly her world had shifted and shrunk six years ago.

'Think of it like Halloween. Only there's an upside. You don't have to return the costume.' Now he picked up the green dress and let it dangle mid-air from the hanger like something broken. 'You can keep it. Keep all of them.' He gestured to the rail. 'And as they're "not who you are", you can sell them. Because they're worth a lot of money and we both know that's what matters to you, isn't it, Sydney?'

In the past she would have kept quiet, tried to defuse the situation, but Tiger had reduced her life, her ambition, her essence, into one cutting rhetorical question. Because as she already knew it was only his opinion that mattered.

'Says the billionaire who stays up until three a.m. working.'

A muscle pulsed in his jaw and he looked as if he might move closer. 'This is going to come as a shock to you, Sydney, but some people actually work hard for a living.'

'I work hard.'

His face was like stone. 'In this instance, working two jobs is not some sign of your diligence. Quite the opposite, in fact. Your position at McIntyre was about deceit and ultimately theft, and all theft is about entitlement and greed.'

'I'm not entitled or greedy.'

'Then why were you stealing from me?'

'I told you I needed—I *need* the money. Or are you deluded enough to think I want to be here with you, that I would for one moment consider pretending to be your girlfriend if you weren't continually threatening to hand me over to the police?'

His eyes were burning a hole in her retinas. He didn't like that, but she didn't care.

'Do you think I want you here?' he said coldly. 'You're just the lesser of two evils.'

That hurt more than it should have done but that wasn't why she flinched. It was the fury in his voice.

'But,' he continued in that same cold voice, 'if this is all such a trial to you, Sydney, then why don't I put you out of your misery and call the police?'

'Because I can't help my brothers if I'm stuck in prison.'

There was a moment of stillness and she knew from the way Tiger was looking at her that her face had gone pale, but she was already spinning on her heel, moving, legs reacting before her brain even knew what she was doing—

She heard Tiger swear, sensed him moving, his hand reaching for her.

'Scusi, signorina.'

Silvana had returned with a trolley laden with boxes and she caught a glimpse of the housekeeper's startled face and then she sidestepped past her and did what she should have done all those years ago when Noah had first made it clear that her feelings didn't matter. That she only mattered in relation to him, and then only if she put his needs above her own.

Never again.

Never.

Again.

Her strides lengthened and as she pushed open a door into the sunshine, she started to run, feet pounding against warm stone, then grass, stumbling, then running, once, then twice. She had no idea where she was going. All she could think about was getting as far away from that scene in the bedroom as possible. She had shown too much emotion, given too much away. Given him more than she had wanted to.

Too late, she realised she should have gone to the jetty, but instead she had reached a beach.

She slowed, slightly out of breath, her heart shuddering against her ribs, her gaze moving past the dancing white-tipped waves to the pale, shimmering city hovering like a mirage beyond it.

Venice.

It was too far away to make out anything specific but even at a distance she felt its calming effect and, a moment later, she reached down and unbuckled her sandals. Pressing her feet into the sand, she felt a wave of homesickness, and guilt. Because she had let them down. Her brothers had needed her and she had failed them.

What had she done?

Tiger was no pussycat, but he wasn't violent. Except his anger, that blind fury she'd heard in his voice and seen on his face, it had panicked her in a way she couldn't control.

It was still rippling through her now, making her want to cry, because it was all such a mess. Being here with him was so far from the worst place she had ever been. But she had been there before and back then she hadn't acted, hadn't defended herself and everything had got so hard, so fast. She hadn't wanted to make the same mistake again.

So she had made a different one.

And there was no point in trying to take it back.

'I don't do second chances, Ms Truitt. You cross me once, we're done.'

Tiger's voice seemed to echo down the beach and, needing to get away from the consequences of her actions, she started to walk beside the tiny, tumbling waves.

Her feet slowed. Set back slightly from the shoreline was a small stone building. It looked too small to be a home, and anyway who would be living there?

Sliding her feet back into her sandals, she walked towards it cautiously, but as she got closer it was obvious it was empty. Abandoned? Tiger had kicked the owners off when he bought the island?

And then as she turned her head a fraction, she saw him. Her stomach plummeted and she lifted a hand to cover her pounding heart.

He was standing there, watching her, his dark head tilted to one side as if he wasn't entirely sure what he was doing there.

He still wasn't sure why he had gone after Sydney, just that watching her leave had pulled at something inside him. Without any kind of conscious decision, he had made his way through the villa and onto the terrace, his gaze fixed on the comet's tail of Sydney's hair.

'It used to be a fisherman's cottage. If that's what you were wondering. It was empty when I came here.'

It was actually one of the main reasons why he had bought this particular island. It was a reminder of how fragile the things you took for granted could be. For years people had pushed their boats away from this shoreline to cast their nets. They had made their homes here, earned a livelihood and then just like that it was gone.

And Venice itself was one of the most perilously situated cities in the world. Anything could be lost and you had to remember that and do anything and everything to stop that from happening.

Sydney was staring at him as if he were a particularly dangerous animal that had escaped from some local zoo and he couldn't really blame her. Even as he had been talking to her, he'd known that he didn't like how he was acting but he'd still been riled by that comment she'd made at breakfast. Casually mentioning how she derailed businesses as if it were nothing. As if she hadn't been planning to do that to him. It was a blunt reminder of who she was, only, with the imprint of that kiss still front and centre in his brain, he had let himself forget.

And then he had expected her to be excited and grateful when he'd shown her the clothes, but she had acted as if it were a bad thing. What woman didn't like new clothes?

Glancing up, he found Sydney watching him, her face pale and still, her hands clenching at her sides.

'Don't let me keep you.' Emotions he couldn't name moved swiftly across her face and he felt a flicker of irritation that he couldn't read them and that she could keep herself out of reach, defying him, even now.

'You know this would be a lot easier if you stopped turning everything into a fight.'

'There is no "this" any more,' she said, lifting her chin in that maddening way of hers.

'Because I bought you some clothes?'

She didn't answer, but she didn't need to. He knew that the clothes were not important. As for the money?

Her hair had come loose and the breeze lifted it away from her small, stiff face, and he held back. Not to savour the moment but because he knew it would hurt her. He knew because he'd heard the hurt in her voice when she had talked about her family.

'Why didn't you tell me?' he said quietly.

'Tell you what?' Her voice was fierce, hostile.

'About your brothers?'

Her skin looked like paper. 'Because people like you think you're different from people like them. Because you don't want to hear that you're the same.'

His heart twisted, which was strange because that particular organ usually functioned solely as a life force but she was so defiant, standing there with her brown eyes.

'What if I did?'

Her hands were like tight balls now and for a moment he thought she wouldn't answer, but then she took a step closer, her eyes narrowing on his face.

'They run a chop shop. They buy and sell stolen parts.' Her voice was fierce, combative, as if defying him to show his disgust, but it only seemed to root him deeper to the spot. 'They do other stuff. Stupid, small-town, small-time stuff with their idiot friends. And now they've been arrested and with their record they're going to go to prison.'

He opened his mouth to speak but she cut across him, fiercer still, 'Let me guess what you're thinking now. The apple doesn't fall far from the tree. Only it's not a tree, is it? The Truitts have a whole orchard. Misdemeanours. Warnings. Arrests. We're all the same. Rotten to the core.'

'You don't know what I'm thinking. We're talking about your brothers and you. And given how much you loathe being here with me, I'm guessing you must love them very much.'

Her eyes were storm dark but there was a tremble to her mouth that made his chest pinch because she was trying to hide her feelings and failing. Only he wasn't sure if it was the trying or failing that felt like a blow.

'I know how it looks but they're not bad people. They just make bad decisions. I don't expect you to understand,' she said after a moment, as if she needed to manage her voice.

But he did understand. Tiger felt his chest tighten. He understood only too well.

She hesitated. 'I didn't mean what I said earlier about being your girlfriend. I mean, obviously I didn't want to do it but you're not who I thought you were.'

Ditto, he thought as she met his gaze.

'Are you going to the police?'

He shook his head. 'But we have to find a way to make this work. We might not be friends but we can't be strangers.'

'I know.' She nodded. 'I could take another look at the clothes.'

'And you could wear some of your own clothes if that would make you feel more comfortable. Or I could get the stylist to select some other options, and you could choose something more "you".'

It was easy to offer that, and he wondered why it had seemed such a point of contention back at the villa. But then that was before he knew the truth. That she wasn't just the grabby little thief he'd assumed her to be. She had a motive, so, yes, she had still tried to steal from him, but at least he understood why. It wasn't greed that had motivated her but love, and loyalty. She had put everything she had on one desperate spin of the roulette wheel. Her job. Her professional reputation. Her freedom. Gazing down into her face, he felt a stab of something like envy. Who would do that for him? Who would sacrifice anything to save him?

He pushed the thought away. This wasn't about him. It was about Sydney, and that look on her face when she'd turned and seen him on the beach. She'd looked like he used to feel. Lost, alone, angry and scared, but trying not to show it and he'd hated it.

'Your brothers, do they have a lawyer?'

'Yes.' She nodded. 'But they need a better one. I did go to the bank, but I'd already taken out a loan to set up the business. And my parents don't have that kind of money. That's why I was trying to hack your system.'

'Then maybe now is a good time to rethink our arrangement, tweak it a little.'

She stared at him warily.

'Look, if you're still willing to help me, then maybe I can help you. I know plenty of good lawyers. I can make some calls, that way your brothers will get proper legal representation.'

Her eyes widened. 'Why would you do that?'

He held her gaze. 'Because you highlighted the vulnerabilities in my system when you hacked it. So, in a way, you did me a favour. Plus, it would be awkward if something came out about your family while we're together, so if I can stop that from happening… I mean, what's the point of being rich if you can't bully and buy your way out of trouble?'

He watched her cheeks flush as she recognised her words.

'That would be such a relief,' she said after a second or two, as if she'd needed a moment to pull herself together, and it wasn't that he was surprised, because he knew her better now, but hearing the tremble in her voice felt like a blow.

'Why did they leave?'

He frowned, then realised she was looking at the stone hut.

'The fishermen? I think it was around the time Venice grew. Other islands were just geographically closer to the city. Times change.'

'It's strange to think that people lived and worked here and then they just disappeared.'

'They didn't take everything. There's some graffiti on the wall.'

Her face shifted then, mouth curving into a smile of such sweetness that he felt momentarily light-headed. 'Here, let me show you.'

He held out his hand and, after a second, she took it and he led her into the hut. Maybe it was because the shutters were closed or perhaps it was the shafts of light slicing through the cool air, but he felt as if he were in a dream.

'Look here.'

Crouching down, she gently touched the writing on the stone. 'What does it say?'

'My Latin is pretty basic but I think it's something about a woman he likes. Wants,' he corrected himself. 'He wants her.'

There was a beat of silence and then she took a step forward into the wavering light and the flush on her cheeks was the realest thing he had ever seen.

CHAPTER SIX

SYDNEY COULD FEEL his heart pounding beneath his ribs.

Tiger hadn't moved but the tiny hut seemed smaller, she seemed closer. But maybe that was because every single one of her senses was homed in on him so that she could practically feel the pulse that was beating haphazardly in his throat. Could see the flecks of both green and amber in the gold of his irises and the unchecked desire. The same desire she knew was mirrored in her eyes.

For a moment, they just stared at one another and then she leaned in or maybe he did, afterwards she couldn't remember, perhaps because it didn't matter. Because they both wanted the same thing.

His mouth on hers. Her lips on his. Soft. Unimaginable. Irresistible.

Miraculous. Because for so long, she had felt neutered, fearful of intimacy and touch, and it felt like a miracle to want sex, to want a man.

No, not a man. This man. She wanted Tiger. And he wanted her.

A shiver of anticipation rippled across her skin as he reached behind her neck and loosened the band, tugging it free so that her hair tumbled down her back.

He slid a hand up to cup her cheek, his touch rough and tender, and she took a shallow breath like a gasp and he pulled back a fraction, but then she pulled him close and he was fitting his mouth to hers, opening her and answering the hunger spilling from her lips.

She had never been kissed like this.

Pleasure was fluttering in her stomach and her lips parted, and she breathed him in, then licked inside his mouth, tasting him on her tongue, her hands tugging at his waistband, fumbling clumsily for the button, then the zip. *Yes*, she thought, as she freed him.

Her head was spinning. He felt amazing. Hard and hot. She could feel the pulse of his blood beating against her fingers.

'Sydney.' He breathed her name against her mouth and the ache in his voice sent something through her, something she had never felt before, something fast and primitive, and she couldn't swallow the whimper rising in her throat.

Jerking his mouth away from hers, he lifted her up onto the window ledge, then dropped to his knees, pushing up the skirt of her dress.

Her heart pounded against her ribcage as he slid her panties down over her legs, then brushed his lips against the triangle of flame-coloured curls. It was like a match meeting kindling. She felt a flare of heat and need and possibility and she moaned then and her hands splayed against his shoulders, pressing down, holding him steady as he flattened his tongue against the pulse beating between her thighs. She rocked against him, moving her hips back and forth.

Heat was swelling inside her; a feverish, dizzying heat

that was changing her, transforming her like alchemy from flesh and bone into something eager and liquid. Her fingers bit into his arm and she was pulling him to his feet.

'Inside me,' she said hoarsely. 'I want you inside me.'

'Are you—?'

'Yes.' She cut him off, her pupils flaring, and he grunted as her fingers curled around him and he slid a hand under her bottom to raise her slightly, using his thumb to part her thighs and then he pushed upwards, entering her smoothly, filling her with heat.

Through the doorway outside, just a few feet away, Tiger could hear the soft rush of the waves as they tumbled onto the beach. The sand, the sea, the breeze…all were there waiting for him.

And it wasn't too late. He could stop this now. He knew that. He had never wanted any woman so much that he couldn't stop and pull back. He had the willpower and the strength of mind to resist.

But he didn't want to resist Sydney.

A groan of pleasure climbed up his throat and out of his mouth and he pressed his knuckles into the rough stone edging the window, leaning into the slight pain, needing it to offset the flickering heat that was rolling through him in waves and stop himself from ending things too fast.

Because even though he badly wanted to let go, he wanted to savour this more.

But then she moaned again, arching against him, her hands seeking his face, panting as she pressed a desperate kiss to his mouth.

He couldn't fight both of them and, clasping her hip,

he began to move, thrusting rhythmically, using his free hand to protect her head as she reared up against him, her muscles tightening around him, spasming again and again, her breath hot and scratchy as she cried out. No longer conscious of the act itself, he clamped her against his shuddering body, surging inside her with molten force to claim her as his own.

He let his head fall forward, breathing raggedly. His skin felt as if it were on fire and he leaned into the damp curve of her throat, his heart raging.

For a few fragmented seconds, neither of them moved, they just clung to one another like survivors of a storm. Then he felt Sydney's hands slide shakily over his torso, almost as if she was checking that he was real and that what had just happened was not some fever dream. And he understood that because he couldn't quite believe that it had happened either.

Finally, he pulled back and out, steadying her as he did so, although he felt less than steady himself.

'I'm fine.'

Her voice momentarily caught him off balance. He had forgotten that they were thinking, speaking creatures, that he was, in fact, a CEO in charge of a global business. Right now, he didn't feel in charge of anything and, glancing down at Sydney, he felt an unfamiliar mix of relief and responsibility as he saw that she looked as shell-shocked as he felt.

Although in some ways, was it that surprising that it had happened?

They had been dancing round that kiss in the kitchen like jittery teenagers. Which was not the image he had of himself ordinarily. There was something about this woman that made him feel younger and less complicated than he had in a long time.

'Excuse me.' She reached past him to pick up her panties, which had somehow ended up on the floor. Now that she was standing up, he could see the stone windowsill and it looked uncomfortably hard and their coupling had all been so frantic, so urgent.

'You're bleeding.'

He frowned. 'What?'

'Your hand.' The softness in her eyes made the dust spirals quiver in the air and he felt suddenly and intensely vulnerable.

'It's nothing.' His voice was harsh, too harsh in that tiny room, but it was an instinctive reaction to feeling anything. Feelings, caring, bonding on anything but a purely physical basis were dangerous. He shrugged. 'I just—'

Just what? His pulse jerked as he remembered the moment when he'd had to push his knuckles into the wall to stop himself from climaxing too soon.

'I caught it on the wall. It's just a scrape. What about you? Are you okay? I didn't hurt you, did I?'

Shaking her head, she smoothed down the skirt of her dress and it was far too easy for him to imagine those slim fingers smoothing other things. As she straightened up, her eyes found his. 'That probably shouldn't have happened.'

'It's a little late to worry about that,' he said softly.

Which was true.

But he didn't have any regrets. That simmering tension between them had been chafing at him and clouding things for sure. No wonder they'd had that stupid bust-up about what she should wear. Now they had got it out of their systems, everything would go more smoothly.

As if their thoughts were running on parallel lines, she said stiffly, 'I don't regret it, but it shouldn't happen again. It was just one of those things.'

He nodded. 'I agree.'

At this point in his life, one-night stands or their daytime equivalent were a little too rogue. He might not be as instantly recognisable as a movie star or pop singer, but having a name like Tiger meant people were more likely to put a value to his face and that made for complications that he didn't need in his life. And this was no different.

Okay, it was different in some ways, he conceded, remembering that hunger that was so unlike any that he'd felt before. It had consumed him and his orgasm was more than just release or relief or ecstasy. It was all those things but it was also a kind of oblivion, and an acknowledgement, a feeling that he was being seen and known completely.

He felt a muscle in his jaw knot. Which was nonsense, of course. Nobody got to know him, he made sure of that.

But this whole arrangement with Sydney was hardly a normal set-up. It was unsurprising, therefore, that he was struggling to make sense of it or that his mind was coming up with left-field explanations.

But really, was it that complicated?

With hindsight, being cooped up with Sydney was obviously going to trip some switches because it was several weeks since he had broken up with Alexandra and sex was a primal need. And while he might have a near mythical status in the business world, he was still just a man.

But this hook-up had scratched the itch, which meant

that now he could concentrate on the week ahead. And afterwards, when she had served her purpose, he would despatch her back to New York on the first flight out of Venice.

Because this didn't change anything, he told himself, feeling calmer than he had for days. It had simply tidied up a few loose ends.

Walking into the bedroom, Sydney shut the door and leaned back against the cool wood, letting it chill her overheated skin.

The beautiful dresses were still hanging from the rail. The window was still slightly open just as she had left it. The curtains were still fluttering in the light, warm sea breeze coming from the lagoon.

Everything looked exactly as it had when she'd stormed out of the room just over an hour ago. Only how could that be?

It should look different. Changed. There should be some external evidence to reflect the transformation inside her because that was what it was. A transformation.

She scowled, suddenly furious. No, it was just sex, she told herself, pushing away from the door and walking across the room to the rail of clothes. Only describing what she and Tiger had just done in the fisherman's hut as just sex was like calling the Sistine Chapel *just* a ceiling.

There had been a moment when she had looked up from that graffiti to find him watching her and she had known that it was a choice. She could choose to walk away if she wanted to.

But everything she'd wanted had been in that room.

And he had wanted her, she thought, her hand closing around the rail. Not to own her or stifle her or simply to prove that he could. He had wanted to kiss and touch and caress and lick—

She felt her thighs clench.

Gazing down at his dark head, she'd felt like a goddess.

But her thoughts had been more prosaic. So that was what the fuss was all about. Because it felt momentous. Miraculous and, oh, so good that she had almost forgotten to breathe.

She still wasn't quite clear on how it had happened. It wasn't as if she'd woken up this morning and thought today would be a good day to have sex.

And she had done more than have sex. She had orgasmed. For the first time in her life.

She had faked it every single time with Noah. He was five years older than her and, coupled with his certainty about everything, that had been thrilling enough for her to ignore the way sex had been mostly uncomfortable and unsatisfactory. For her anyway. Which he had made clear was her fault, not his.

She knew what passion was now, and pleasure. What was less clear was why her body had chosen to discover both those things with Tiger McIntyre.

It wasn't that unclear, she thought, her pulse twitching as she pictured Tiger's astonishing face. He was beautiful, undeniably so with those flawless contoured features and those mesmerising gold eyes. Plus, he clearly knew what he was doing when it came sex. Only it was more than just technical expertise—he had wanted to please her.

And before that, he had wanted to make sure she was okay.

She felt her body tense at the memory of when she'd realised he had come after her. With Noah, running, hiding from him, had always been a last resort. Mostly she'd just wanted it over with, but also it would increase his rage tenfold.

'Don't make me have to look for you—' he would threaten down the phone on his way home. And sometimes she hadn't. But other times she hadn't been able to stop herself.

A shiver ran over her skin.

Her body had taken charge just as it had in the bedroom with Tiger. Because she'd thought she had gone too far, pushed him too far, and he had been angry, and exasperated, but he'd been controlling his anger. It hadn't been controlling him.

Instead of raging he had asked questions and listened to her answers. They'd had a conversation, and that in a way felt as climatic as her very first orgasm.

She trailed her fingers over the smooth silk, remembering the smoothness of his skin. It was a lot to take in, but not as much as she had revealed. Was it too much? It was certainly more than she had ever shared or wanted to share before. Even just the thought of doing so had made her feel naked, flayed by the curiosity and judgement in people's eyes, but Tiger hadn't judged.

There had been an intensity to his focus, as if he couldn't look away, as if he'd liked what he'd seen and she had liked the way he'd looked at her. Of course, back in the States it would be different. In the real world, she wasn't ready to let someone get close, but this wasn't real, and maybe that was why she had felt safe enough to open herself to Tiger physically and emotionally.

* * *

Gazing up at the pale sun that was sliding smoothly up through the cloudless blue sky, Tiger checked the timer on his watch. Two minutes left.

Easy, he thought, accelerating across the grass to the beach and the shimmering sea.

He had slept badly then woken early and decided to run around the island. Because why not? The sun was shining. There was a soft, warm breeze. It was going to be a beautiful day, which was good news because today was the day of the Regata Storica.

It was also, give or take, eighteen hours since he had been inside Sydney's body.

He swore as he lost his footing and stumbled forward onto the sand. Because it wasn't the first time he had lost his footing over the last eighteen hours, metaphorically speaking at least. And the reason for his clumsiness was no doubt still sleeping. In his bed.

Gritting his teeth, he glanced at his watch. That stumble had cost him thirty seconds. Which meant that now he could add time to the list of things that Sydney Truitt had stolen or tried to steal from him.

Walking back to the villa with her yesterday morning, he had confidently assumed that things would go back to normal. Normal being a state where he had already moved on. Variety was good, and control. Relationships, for want of a better word, only happened on his terms, so when Sydney had said that they shouldn't have sex again, he had been completely on board with that.

Or so he'd thought.

Everything had been fine at first. Over lunch, he'd felt calm, relaxed even, but then his body had still been suffused with post-coital endorphins. Then afterwards, Sydney had disappeared upstairs to try on some of the clothes and he had taken some calls from work, but he had found it difficult to concentrate because he could see Sydney from the window of his office. She'd been sitting by the pool, and most women, particularly a woman he'd just had sex with, would be not just wearing a bikini but languidly smoothing sun lotion on herself. He'd seen it all so many times. And the more they tried to tempt him, the less interested he got.

Because he wasn't Gerald McIntyre.

Not even close.

Only Sydney hadn't been rubbing sun cream onto her skin. Nor had she been wearing a bikini. She had been not quite fully dressed, but not far off it, and yet he hadn't been able to look away. He kept remembering the parts of her body he had so briefly glimpsed when they had reached for one another in the half-light of the fisherman's hut.

The curve of her shoulder. That doe-soft skin of her inner thighs. The pale swell of her breast.

But that was it. That was all he was going to get. A glimpse, because Sydney was not looking for anything to happen again.

Was that why she had got under his skin and into his dreams? That was certainly a first for him, this feeling of wanting more. He had never wanted to be the kind of man who could be controlled by his desires, because that would take him dangerously close to becoming like his father.

But despite this arrangement supposedly being on his

terms, Sydney seemed to be full of ways to make him question who he was and what he wanted.

The trouble was he knew what he wanted.

He felt his legs slow beneath him.

It was strange to admit it, given that he'd had any number of sexual partners since he'd lost his virginity in high school, but he had forgotten how pleasurable sex could be. For as long as he could remember, sex had been about satisfying a physical need.

And yet here he was, up at dawn after a night spent feverishly stripping Sydney in his dreams, his body hard and aching and jangling with a need that he couldn't still or stifle, and it felt very personal.

But that would change today, he realised with a rush of relief. The regatta was always rammed. They would be surrounded by people and after the regatta there was lunch and then cocktails and dinner so, basically, the opposite of personal.

Looking down at his watch, he stopped and reset the timer. If he ran fast enough, he would still have time to lap the island and shower before they had to leave. It would be cutting it fine but that was what he did, who he was. He didn't just meet, he welcomed a challenge, and, starting the timer again, he began to run.

Shifting back against the leather upholstery, Tiger gazed at the brilliant, saturated blue water as Angelo guided the speedboat across the waves. The lagoon had its own unique character. It was part of the Adriatic and yet it was separated from the vast expanse of sea, protected by seawalls and the prayers of the population. To him, it felt like an oasis, and Sydney clearly thought so too.

He let his gaze drift over to where she was looking across the water, transfixed almost.

'Are you okay? I can get Angelo to slow down.'

She turned, her forehead creasing above her nose. 'Why would he do that?'

'I thought you might be feeling sick. You didn't eat much at breakfast.'

Her eyes found his, startled, the soft brown irises huge in the sunlight. 'No, I'm fine. I was—' She gave him a small, stiff smile. 'I *am* a bit nervous, but I don't feel sick.'

'Don't be nervous. You've got this.' His eyes moved over her face then dropped to her short-sleeved silk shirt in wide horizontal stripes of sky blue and white and the pleated blue skirt she was wearing. She had put her hair up in some kind of soft, muddled updo and the whole effect was very pretty, very sexy.

'So stop worrying and enjoy the view.'

He watched her head turn. Her lips parted.

'Welcome to Venice,' he said softly.

Her smile snagged at his senses. 'I couldn't really see it properly when we arrived because it was dark.' In the sunlight, she looked excited, her nerves forgotten. 'It doesn't look real. It looks like a mirage.'

'I know what you mean. But we're still some way out. Up close, it will all feel a lot more real.'

Tiger was right, Sydney thought as they made their way through the palazzo to the balcony where they would be watching the races. There were a lot of people. More people than she had ever seen in one place and the noise and the energy felt in-your-face real.

As they walked towards the sponsors' balcony, Tiger was welcomed like a returning monarch, fresh from a victorious battle, although, so far, he hadn't introduced her to anyone. Not that it mattered. He was the one they wanted to get close to, and it seemed as if everybody wanted to greet him and, although she had been telling the truth when she said that she didn't feel sick, she felt dazed by this sudden reminder that he was a big deal. The main event.

He looked the part, all golden eyes and tanned skin and yet another suit that fitted every curve and angle of his body. She wasn't the only one to notice either. Women watched him like hawks. Except that made him sound as though he were a rabbit or a mouse, and he was neither. He was a tiger.

'Tiger, how are you? I thought I heard screaming.' A dark-haired man wearing an artfully crumpled linen suit grabbed Tiger by the arm and pumped his hand enthusiastically. 'I heard you were a sponsor this year. Thought I might see you here for the film festival. Lot of beautiful women—'

He glanced at Sydney as if seeing her for the first time, his eyes narrowing appreciatively. 'But I see you're already covered in that department. Scotty Aldridge, and you are?'

'Heading out to watch the races. Gotta watch my team,' Tiger said smoothly, cupping Sydney's elbow in his hand and sidestepping her past Scotty Aldridge as he leaned forward.

'Is there a problem?'

Tiger frowned. 'What do you mean?'

'You haven't introduced me to anyone. I might as well not be here.' It shouldn't matter. This wasn't real. He wasn't her 'boyfriend', but he had been off with her.

She glanced down at her blouse and skirt. 'Is it what I'm wearing? Do you not like it?'

'I do. I did. I should have said something before. I wanted to,' he said. 'You look beautiful. Too beautiful to be pawed by some man old enough to be your father.'

She bit her lip. 'My grandfather, actually. My dad got my mum pregnant when they were fifteen. It was a shotgun wedding. No, really, her brothers turned up with actual shotguns.'

'Is that a family tradition? I mean, should I be expecting your brothers to roll up at some point?'

'That would be unlikely.' She gave him a small lopsided smile. 'As I haven't told them about us. I haven't told anyone about us.'

He raised an eyebrow. 'And there you were accusing me of being ashamed of being seen with you.'

'I didn't accuse you of that,' she protested as he took her hand and pulled her closer.

'You were thinking it,' he said softly. 'How could I be ashamed? You look beautiful. You are beautiful.' His eyes were dark and steady on her face, and it would be easy to believe him, and for a moment she did. But, of course, he was just saying the kind of things a man would say to his girlfriend.

'You don't believe me?'

'I feel like an imposter. But I suppose you think that's some kind of hubris.'

'What I think is that you're talking nonsense. Every single person in this room is playing a part. Everyone has a hidden agenda. So just because you and I have one, doesn't mean you don't belong. And you are beautiful, Sydney.'

His words made her feel light-headed. Noah had made her feel so ugly and worthless. He had made her believe that she was the problem. That everyone saw what he saw, and that it wasn't good enough. And she knew that wasn't true but hearing Tiger say it out loud made her feel as if she were filling with light that was brighter and warmer than the sun.

'I wanted to tell you before but Silvana and the maids were there and I thought it would look as if I was doing it for their benefit. But I thought it, I still do. You believe me, don't you?'

And the crazy thing was, she did. Because Tiger didn't need to say it. They'd already had sex. Nor did he need to keep her sweet, because theirs was a finite, transactional arrangement. But most important of all, she could see the admiration in his gaze, feel it as it touched her skin, hot and bright like the lick of a flame.

Impulsively she leaned forward and kissed him. For a second, she felt his body tense with surprise and then he was kissing her back, and the heat and the noise from the regatta felt like a separate place.

Her lips parted and she felt his tongue, and she made a soft noise against his mouth as his hand moved to the nape of her neck, and she felt his thumb, sure and firm, holding her steady, which was lucky because her legs were all out of steadiness.

'Get a room, McIntyre,' someone shouted and she pulled

back, her breath jerking in her throat, her hands tight in his shirt.

Tiger's eyes held and for a moment he just stared at her, breathing unsteadily, as if he was as thrown by the taste of her as she was by him.

'We should go and watch the race,' he said finally.

'Yes, we should.'

The balcony was heaving with people but the crowds parted like the waves for Tiger and he guided her to the far left corner.

'You'll get the best view here.'

'Can you see? It's your boat.'

'I can see everything I want to,' he said softly, moving behind her, his hand resting on her waist.

She barely noticed how many boats there were or who won. She was only aware of the places where Tiger's body grazed hers. Her waist. Her hip. Her throat when he leaned in to kiss her neck and she leaned back into him, her breath catching as he held her close.

'This is our race,' he said finally as another cluster of boats waited for the starter's gun to fire. 'Can you tell which one is our crew?'

That was easy. Even among the bright colours, the orange and black of *The McIntyre* stood out. There was a band and the crowd roared as the crews began rowing smoothly through the rippling blue water.

Behind her, Tiger was still, but she could feel his tension beneath her own quivering excitement.

'They won. You won.' She turned towards him as the balcony erupted into cheers, her chest tight and swollen with pride and happiness and then Tiger was kissing her fiercely.

'You won,' she said again as he broke the kiss and pulled her against his chest.

He was pleased but he shook his head. 'They won. I paid.'

They watched the last race and then everyone started to drift downstairs.

'What happens now?' she whispered.

'Drinks, canapés, a lot of pointless conversation.'

'*Scusi.*' A beautiful dark-haired woman glanced up from her phone, smiling approvingly, her cat's eyes flaring at the corner as she caught sight of Tiger. 'No, darling. Let's go to Corbucci's. I heard Harris Carver was there and I want to see if he's as delectable in person as everyone claims.'

Sydney felt her face freeze.

Harris Carver.

He was here.

She felt sick. Looked sick too, she realised a moment later as she looked up and found Tiger staring at her steadily.

'You know Harris Carver.' His eyes were narrowing, and she could sense him moving pieces of a puzzle around, turning them, rearranging them.

'Signor McIntyre, would you like to join the winning teams for a photo?'

It was one of the event organisers, beaming.

'I would.' Tiger cut him off smoothly. 'But unfortunately something has come up. Another time maybe.'

His arm tightened around her waist and he began to frogmarch her through the crowd.

'We don't have to leave.'

He jerked her round to face him. 'Oh, but we do. You see, I saw your face back there. You know Harris Carver, and right now all that matters to me is finding out how.'

CHAPTER SEVEN

THE JOURNEY BACK to the island seemed to take no time at all.

As Angelo slowed alongside the jetty, Tiger was already out of the speedboat, pulling her up alongside him and guiding her back towards the villa.

Silvana was waiting for them in the entrance hall but as she stepped forward to greet them she caught sight of her boss's face and changed her mind.

'In here.' Tiger threw open the door to his office and Sydney followed him in, her breath catching in her throat as he stalked past her and turned to face her.

Today in the sunshine with the cheers of the spectators echoing around them as the McIntyre *gondolino* had crossed the finishing line first, she had forgotten this was how it had started. Gazing up into his golden eyes, she'd been lulled into a false sense of security, but Tiger and Harris Carver moved in the same circles and now it felt inevitable that his name should have come up.

'Sit. Talk. Now,' he ordered, folding his arms in front of his body and lifting his chin in that commanding, autocratic way of his. He was practically vibrating with a mix of fury and disbelief so in that sense it was more or less a replay of what had happened in the New York office, except she could see the sea here through the windows and there were no burly security guards hovering at the margins of her vision.

She sat down, her heart thumping jerkily.

This wasn't like before when they had argued about the clothes. Then, his anger had been hot and blurred at the edges with exasperation, and her survival instincts had kicked in and overridden everything so that even though she wasn't physically scared of Tiger, she'd had to run.

But she didn't want to run now.

What she wanted was for things to go back to how they had been at the regatta when he had stood slightly behind her to watch the race, his hands resting on her hips, anchoring her to him, his stubble grazing her skin as he'd leaned in to kiss her softly at the base of her neck.

She stared at him, dry-mouthed, trying to calm her beating heart. He didn't look as if he wanted to kiss her now.

He looked distant. Hostile. And when he spoke, his voice scraped over her like sandpaper. 'Do you think that silence is going to save you? That if you stall for long enough, I'll give up? I won't, I promise you. So why don't you stop wasting my time and tell me how you know Harris Carver?'

'I only met him once.'

'When?' He bit the question off and spat it at her.

'About ten days before I came to work for you.' She swallowed, her brief, unsettling rendezvous with Harris Carver flashing across her mind, so real and vivid that for an instant she could smell the leather of the club armchair and feel its smooth warmth against her back.

'What happened in between?'

'With him? Nothing. I just told you. I only met him once.'

'You've told me a lot of things, Sydney. Most of them are either untrue or a partial truth so I'm sure you'll understand my reluctance to take you at your word.'

His voice was taut and strained. 'Why didn't you tell me all this back in New York? Or out on the beach? I thought we had some kind of understanding, but you were lying to me and you'd still be lying to me now if somebody hadn't mentioned Carver's name. I mean, when were you going to tell me?'

She swallowed.

'I met him once,' she repeated. 'There was no reason to meet him again. But I needed the time in between to create my identity and references.'

'Sounds like you know what you're doing.' Her throat tightened as Tiger's eyes jerked to hers. 'So, the cybersecurity company of yours is a front. This is what you do. You tout your hacking services to billionaires. Steal on demand.' His eyes narrowed, and the air in the room snapped tight. 'Does he know about this? About you being here with me?'

'No.' She shook her head. 'He doesn't. I haven't told anyone. And I don't steal on demand. I've never—'

'Stolen anything,' he finished her sentence and the sneer in his voice made something curl up inside her. 'I remember. Back in New York when I confronted you, you said, "This is the first time I've done anything like this," and I didn't believe you. But then I found out about your brothers and I thought you might be telling the truth. But you were lying then and you're lying now, aren't you?'

No, and yes. No, she had never hacked anyone and stolen

their IP, but yes, she had done something even more reck-less and dangerous. She had taken her ex-husband's phone.

So tell him. Tell him what you stole.

But she couldn't, because that would mean telling him why she had stolen the phone. Which would mean telling him about Noah and opening up a can of worms, opening herself up so that he would see the ugliness of the scars that hadn't faded, laying bare her stupidity and weakness.

And she didn't know why but the idea of him seeing that, knowing that about her, felt like the very worst thing she could imagine right now.

'It's not what you're thinking,' she said quietly.

'The trouble is,' he said after a moment that seemed to last a lifetime, 'everything I know about you tells me that it is exactly what I'm thinking.'

Her hands clenched. 'He approached me. Harris Carver. His people got in touch with me. It was all very hush-hush. I had to sign an NDA and they picked me and took me to some private members' club.'

He frowned. 'You mean the Millenium?'

'I don't know. We went in via some underground car park. I didn't see anybody except a man in a suit who showed us where to go.'

Tiger reached back and switched on the light on his desk and she had a sudden sharp memory of a different lamp on a different desk and a moment in time that had snapped through her like a lightning strike and left her singed and shaking inside.

'I didn't know what he wanted me to do when I agreed to meet him. I thought he was going to offer me a job. A job at HCI.'

'You wanted to work for him?' His eyes blazed, and if theirs had been a different kind of relationship she might have thought there was a jealousy to his temper.

'Not him. His business. I needed money and HCI is an S&P 500 company.'

'Right, and he's so squeaky clean, isn't he? Harris Carver: all-round good guy.'

She thought back to that nerve-racking meeting and Carver's steady grey gaze. 'No, I didn't think he was a good guy. I felt like I was swimming in a tank with a shark the whole time I was there.'

'But he made you an offer you couldn't refuse.'

'I did refuse it. I told him that I wasn't comfortable doing what he wanted. But it was a lot of money for three days' work.'

'Work?' His mouth twisted into a shape that made it hard to breathe. 'For the last time, what you did wasn't work. It was theft. Here.'

She blinked. Tiger was holding out the flash drive he had taken from her. 'But I'm guessing my word counts for nothing alongside Saint Carver's, so why don't you take a look? See for yourself.'

His anger was different this time. It felt older, and bitter, as if it had been left to fester. As if he, not Carver, had been wronged.

He pushed away from the desk and walked towards the window and after a moment she got up and sat down in front of his laptop and pushed in the flash drive.

Somebody, possibly Tiger's head of IT, had finished running the program she had set up and she clicked through the images on the screen. They were all of some kind of drill bit. More importantly, there was a tiger's head stamped across each image: the tiger's head trademark of the Mc-Intyre Corporation.

Her head was spinning. She sucked in a breath. 'This is your property?'

'Correct.' Tiger nodded.

'So you didn't steal this from HCI.' Which meant that things were back to front. Black was white. Day was night and she wasn't some caped crusader righting wrongs, but simply the thief Tiger had accused her of being.

And all because she had taken Harris Carver's words at face value.

Obviously, she had heard of Tiger, but, up until that meeting with Carver, everything she'd known about him had been based on the third-hand gossip and hearsay and rumours that swirled around the Internet.

But Harris moved in the same circles and he had confirmed what she'd already believed to be true. That Tiger McIntyre was just another fat cat, or, in his case, a lean, muscular big cat who played the system and thought the rules applied to everyone else. So, stealing back something that belonged to someone else had felt more like meting out natural justice than theft.

And then there was the money.

With hot, slippery panic swelling inside her every time she thought about her brothers, she had been eager to find a benefactor. And Harris Carver had known that. That was why he had shown her the amount he was prepared to pay her, because he'd known that seeing it made it real, made it feel as if it were already hers, and then it was that much harder to say no.

It was basic psychology. Fish and bait. Donkey and carrot. *Basic.*

But effective.

And the depressing truth was that it was most effective on the people like her who were desperate to ignore the fact that the wriggling worm was on a hook on the end of a line attached to a rod held by a fisherman.

'Doesn't feel good, does it? Being deceived? Played?' Tiger's gaze felt like an insistent, living thing tearing and mauling her and for the first time she wondered if she had completely misunderstood what had happened when she'd sat down in that quiet, wood-panelled room.

'Because that's what happened. Carver saw that you were someone who could be turned and so he lied to you and used you.'

His words echoed around the room, stark and undeniable, and she shivered inside because Noah had seen something in her too. A weakness, a vulnerability, a need to be something more than the rest of her family and he had exploited it, flattering her, offering a future away from petty crime and financial insecurity, then isolating her and slowly taking her off the bone.

And she had always thought that a part of why her exhusband had targeted her was her youth and her hunger to be something more than just another Truitt clogging up the courts.

But she wasn't eighteen any more. She was nearly twenty-five. She owned her own, admittedly small business, but it was still hers. And a year of marriage to Noah had taught her enough about the dark side of life to immunise her against lowering her guard. Curled up on the back seat of Connor's pick-up, she had made a promise to build her barricades high.

Only then Harris Carver had come along with his money and his offer of a way out just as Noah had, and she hadn't questioned his opinions or his motivations. At least not enough to stop herself from making a bad situation worse.

'He did use me,' she said slowly.

She could see that now, and yet she could still see Carver's face, see that shadow of something that was darker, deeper, weightier than professional rivalry. It hadn't been important then. What had she cared about the cause of their conflict? Now, though, it seemed to matter a lot.

'But I don't think he lied to me. In fact, I know he didn't. He believed what he was saying.'

Tiger's face stiffened. 'Because he's the hero of this story, right?' he said, and the harshness in his voice made her chest tighten. 'Let me guess, you started believing him right after he told you how much he was going to pay you.'

'No,' she protested. 'That's not true.' Except in a way it was, she thought, replaying the timeline of that conversation with Carver. And Tiger, of course, correctly interpreted that realisation on her face.

'It's amazing how convincing money can be,' he said, and the steel beneath the softness in his voice was so ferocious that it sharpened something inside her.

'It wasn't just about the money. I thought I was righting a wrong.'

Two weeks ago, she had been so sure of Carver's story but now those certainties were collapsing. And yet there was still something nagging at her.

'That was what he said to me,' she said after a moment. 'That he wanted me to take something back from you.'

'And now you know he was lying.'

She did. But somewhere inside her head she could hear that note in Carver's voice when he'd told her that Tiger was no angel.

'About the IP, yes, but then he said that it wasn't the first time you'd stolen from him. Only that was after I'd already agreed to work for him. He didn't need to give me another reason, so why did he?'

'I don't know. More importantly, I don't care.'

Except he did, she realised. She could see it in the sudden stiffening of his shoulders, and she remembered the comment that woman had made after the race, the one that had started off this whole inquisition.

'Carver said it was personal between you two.'

Tiger straightened. 'But this, you and I, we aren't,' he said coolly. 'We might have held hands and kissed and looked into each other's eyes all afternoon but that was a performance. You are not my girlfriend. You're the hired help. And your services are no longer required.'

She stared at him in disbelief, fighting for control. 'You're sacking me? No, that isn't going to happen. You don't get to drag me halfway round the world just to dump me over some detail—'

'Detail.' His features contorted. 'This is not a detail. And we are done here.'

He stalked past her, and she watched him go, her body rooted to the floor with frustration and disbelief, her brain somehow still conscious of the lethal, masculine grace with which he moved despite his anger.

And he was angry.

His anger felt defensive, almost as if he needed to keep her at arm's length.

She knew that feeling, that need to have high walls around her. Make that high walls and a moat. It was how she had lived her life for five years. Until Tiger had gone to look for her the other day. Not to have the last word. Or to punish her. Or make her 'see sense', and if that didn't work, then make her see stars. He had wanted to make sure she was okay.

Didn't he deserve the same level of care?

She didn't have to stay with him, just check that he was all right.

The house was quiet, just as it had been that first night when she'd crept downstairs in the darkness to find something to eat, but Tiger wasn't in the kitchen. Nor was he in the living room or in his bedroom or any of the other rooms. Which meant he must be outside, somewhere on the island.

Through the window, the sun was slowly sinking towards the horizon. It would be dark soon and she wasn't a big fan of the dark. But for some reason she wasn't frightened here on the island. She felt oddly safe.

The air was still warm but it would be cool soon and she ducked back into the villa and grabbed a throw from the sofas. Outside, she slipped off her espadrilles. There was no sign of him on the terrace or in the tented gazebo at the edge of the lawn.

Could he have left the island? She made her way down to where the speedboat was moored, and that was when she saw him, standing at the end of the jetty, his elbows resting on the balustrade, his head bowed over the water. He had rolled up his sleeves and lost the loafers and he looked like a model doing a photoshoot for some upmarket clothing brand or watch.

'Why are you still here? Didn't you get the message?'

She froze. Even though she was barefooted, he had heard her, but he spoke without looking up at her, which made it easier to keep walking towards him.

'That you fired me? Yeah, I got that. But I just wanted to make sure you were okay.'

He looked over then. 'You don't need to pretend any more, Sydney, and I think we both know that you don't give a damn whether I'm okay.'

'I never had to pretend in private.'

'I'm fine. Go back inside, it'll be cold soon.'

'I know. That's why I brought you this.' She held out the throw, which he ignored, and, after a moment, she draped it over the balustrade, then rested her hands against the smooth rail.

A muscle pulsed in his jaw and there was that note of impatience in his voice. 'I told you to go inside.'

'I will if you will.'

It was the first thing that came into her head. Her brothers always used to say it to one another when they were younger and they were daring each other to do something stupid or dangerous or both. Her throat tightened as Tiger looked over at her, his golden eyes dark and narrow, and she wondered which category this fell into.

'What are you? A child? Go back to the villa.'

'What are you? My dad?'

There wasn't a flicker of reaction on his flawless face or even in those dark gold eyes, but she felt the air snap tight. 'Clearly not. If I were, you wouldn't be earning a living committing cyber crimes or spending your evenings sipping whisky with random men who pay you to commit those crimes.'

'Crime,' she said quietly.

His eyes locked onto hers. 'I'm not sure that makes an awful lot of difference in law.'

'I think it does. It's my first offence and there were extenuating circumstances.'

'I don't think greed qualifies.'

She changed tack. 'What about coercion? Blackmail? What does the law think about that?'

'Whatever I tell it to think.' He was staring at her, a flare of incredulity lighting up his eyes. 'Are you seriously threatening me?'

'Yes. No.' She fought to keep her voice steady. 'I don't know, Tiger. I've never done this before. I don't even know what this is.'

'This is you throwing away your life for a man who doesn't even value your sacrifice.'

'I didn't do it for him. I did it for my brothers.'

There was a long silence. Tiger stared past her, his chest lifting and rising infinitesimally.

'Sometimes you can't save people. Sometimes they don't want to be saved. Or maybe you don't have what it takes to save them. Sometimes all you can do is protect yourself.'

Yes, she thought, remembering the moment when she had called Connor. It was as if Tiger knew. She was suddenly shaking inside and there was a tense silence broken only by the water lapping gently against the jetty.

But she didn't notice the silence or the water. She was

too transfixed by his taut silhouette because Tiger wasn't talking about her and her brothers. He was talking about himself, and that jolted her, only it was so snarled up with the tumult of emotions swirling inside her that it took a moment for her to reply.

'Sometimes you can't even do that.'

Tiger breathed out unsteadily, Sydney's words drowning out the world so that the breeze coming off the water grew still and the jetty and the speedboat and the balustrade seemed to lose shape and fade into the darkening light. Only the woman standing beside him stayed vivid and as sharply drawn as a pen-and-ink sketch on vellum.

'Sometimes.' Make that never, he thought, remembering his father's last, bedridden days, and he felt that same helplessness and sense of waste and loss, and anger. Always anger.

'They can be hard to bear, those times.'

A ripple of water lifted the jetty and he felt it judder through his bones as he shrugged. 'It doesn't matter.' He wouldn't allow it to matter.

He felt her move closer and he wanted to touch her then, wanted to touch her so much, to pull her close and not feel alone. Only that was the reason he couldn't, shouldn't.

To need Sydney like that, not for sex but because she was the only person who could soothe the ache in his chest, would be a sign of weakness and for so long now he had resisted emotional entanglement.

But Sydney had followed, and he was no longer alone. And he found that he didn't want her to go, not when her brown eyes were steadying him as she waited for him to speak, and he was more than tempted, he was struggling to hold back.

That she was here, and that she cared about him enough to put her own feelings aside, stunned him, and swept away the anger that he could now acknowledge was disproportionate and misplaced. She had scraped against a poorly healed wound, but it was Harris who had caused that wound. And it was partly that he had never called him to account that rankled, but also it had stung, finding out that Sydney had this connection with the man who had cast his friendship aside, and over a woman.

More than stung, it had hurt a lot. On more levels than he cared to acknowledge.

And in that moment, he hated that he'd revealed that hurt to Sydney.

But what was worse than all of that put together was knowing that he was no better than Harris. They had both spotted a vulnerability in Sydney and exploited it, and knowing that made him want to smash things.

'It does matter. You matter,' she said in that quiet, husky way of hers and everything tilted sideways as if the jetty were moving beneath them, but he knew that it was him. He was unmoored.

'It doesn't change anything though, does it?' he said, almost angrily because, more than anything, he wanted to believe what she was saying. Wanted it more than anything he had ever wanted, only that would mean straying from the path he'd chosen and following in his father's footsteps.

'If you mean the past, then no, you can't change that. But you can change how you feel about the past.'

'I doubt that.'

'Why?' Her beautiful brown eyes were narrow and dark on his face. 'Because that might mean you were wrong?'

'No, because every time I think about my father, I want to punch things.' He hadn't been going to say that, but the words came out in a rush as if they had been sitting there, just waiting to be spoken.

She blinked, and he felt her body tense beside him. 'Did he hurt you?'

'Hurt me? You mean hit me? No.' He shook his head, appalled. And yet, the answer to her question was yes, he realised, or how else could he explain that dark ache inside his chest that he had carried for so long?

'There are other ways to be hurt by someone.'

'I don't think he knew he was hurting me. Not in the beginning anyway. After my mother died, he was adrift. He couldn't be on his own, and every single time he was so sure that he was in love, so sure they were in love with him, even when it was completely obvious that it wouldn't last.'

'How many times were there?'

'Six. But I only really had to deal with the first four. I went to college just before he married number five.'

'Didn't any of them last?'

'I think the longest was probably four years. She was number three. A couple of them lasted around six months. There was one who lasted three weeks. You would have thought he'd learn from his mistakes but he never did. He'd meet them and he'd be so sure they were the one and the next thing they'd be married and then they would divorce him and he'd be on to the next one.'

'But he loved them?'

'He thought he did. But it always fell apart so easily. And

each divorce left him a little poorer but not a little wiser.' His mouth twisted. 'In the end it was just a mess. He had to sell our home and downsize and he did that again and again until there was nothing left. It was the same with the business, although I managed to hold onto one mine and the name.'

'And where did you fit in?'

'I didn't.' It was the first time he'd ever admitted that to anyone. 'None of my stepmothers really wanted me around. And my father was either distracted or desolate. It wasn't all bad. I mean, I had a roof over my head and there was food on the table and he was smart and funny, and I loved him. I loved who he used to be.'

Gazing down at Sydney, he remembered that ache in her voice when she'd asked him what he wouldn't do to save someone he cared about. The answer was simple. If it meant saving his father from his worst impulses, he would have sold his soul.

'That must have been hard.'

It had been such a long time since anyone had been there for him. Obviously he could draw on the expertise of his staff if he needed financial or legal advice, but he had never been able to let people get close to him.

He'd seen the consequences too many times with his father and then the one time he'd thought he had found someone he could trust, it had blown up in his face.

'School was tough. It was a small town. You know what they're like. Everybody knows everyone else's business. My dad was a great go-to for gossip. What is it they say? No fool like an old fool? And I was the old fool's son.

'I got a lot of grief from the other kids, and I was on a

pretty short fuse so I was a bit of a loner. And then I got a place at MIT, and nobody knew who I was or who my dad was and what he'd done. I guess I relaxed a bit. That's when I met Harris.'

'You were at university together?'

'He was in the same halls as me and we just clicked. We had the same interests, same determination, same focus. We were really competitive, but in a good way. We drove each other on. I don't have siblings, but he felt like a brother to me.'

Sydney felt her stomach twist. There was a tension to Tiger's spine that looked painful.

'What happened?'

'He had a lot of girlfriends, we both did. Nothing serious or exclusive. He dated some of my exes and I hooked up with some of his. You know how it is?'

No, she thought. Her sex life had been nothing like Tiger's casual 'friends with benefits' approach to relationships. It had been tense and confusing and limited to one man's view of what it should be.

'But it wasn't like that with Franny. I knew she was different. That they were seeing each other. Anyway, my dad was ill a lot that year and I had to go home because his last wife had left him and he was on his own, and when I got back, she was in my bed.'

Sydney felt a stab of jealousy that was as sharp as it was irrational.

'My roommate had let her in. Apparently, she and Harris had fallen out and she wanted to talk to me about him. I tried but I wasn't, I'm *not*, good at talking about relationships. Anyway, she was tired and I had classes so I told her she could stay and get her head straight. She came to the door to see me off, and she must have taken one of my T-shirts to sleep in. Long story short, Harris saw us.'

'Didn't you tell him what happened?'

A muscle tightened in his jaw. 'He didn't give me a chance. He followed me downstairs and punched me in the face and I lost my temper because it hurt and so I hit him back.'

He pressed the heel of his hand against his forehead. 'Someone called Security and we both got hauled up in front of the dean and Harris said I started it.'

Sydney could hear the pain in his voice. 'Why did he do that?'

'I suppose he thought I'd slept with his girlfriend. The stupid thing is, if we'd both taken a step back things might have been different, but he was angry and I was too angry to back down.' He tipped back his head. 'I didn't know how to back down, so I said a few stupid things and then a couple more just to make sure I messed things up real good and got myself kicked out.'

'What happened to Carver?'

'Nothing. He finished his degree. I didn't see him again for years. Didn't think I ever would but suddenly he was in New York and now our paths cross all the time. Not literally, just we run in the same circles, bid for the same contracts.'

'He needs someone to put him right.'

Glancing down at her clenched fists, he almost smiled.

'Yeah, but not you. I can deal with him.' He unpeeled her fingers and slotted his hand into hers. She felt his gaze on her face. 'I'm the bad guy here, remember? Bullying and buying my way out of trouble.'

She blinked. He was smiling now, that absurd, astonishing smile that made something tug loose inside. 'I might have jumped to some wrong conclusions.'

'I think we're both guilty of that.' He fell silent. 'I miss my father,' he said after a moment. 'Weirdly, I miss Harris too. We were on the same page. I trusted him. But then it was like I was disposable.' There was an ache to this voice then, and she knew why he had reacted in that moment. That punch was the culmination of abandonment, grief for everything he'd lost, all mixed up with the defiance of that small boy who'd had to take on all comers.

But it wasn't vicious or punitive. Tiger could be ruthless and determined but, even in the beginning, he had shown restraint.

'After that, I kind of shut down. I decided it was easier to "walk by my wild lone".' Catching sight of her face, he smiled stiffly. 'It's a quote from this book my grandmother used to read to me. It's about why cats don't trust dogs and why they keep their distance from humans. I guess I sympathise.'

'You didn't deserve any of what happened to you,' she said slowly. 'You didn't do anything wrong. You were a child and your dad thought that meant your feelings were less important than his. But you also said he was adrift. Maybe love always seemed like a risk worth taking. Maybe he saw marriage as an anchor, for you as well as him.'

'Maybe,' he said slowly. 'I think he wanted that; he just went about it all wrong. He kind of said that before he died but I wasn't ready to listen.'

'But you were there for him when he needed you.'

She squeezed his hand, and after a moment he pulled her closer, close enough that their foreheads were touching.

'You know there's not many businesses that could handle this kind of specialist equipment. HCI and McIntyre basically slug it out over the big contracts. That's why we often end up going down the same path, so when I thought about who might be a buyer, I did think of Harris, but I thought you'd have to approach him. I didn't think he was the person who'd set it in motion. Only then I saw your face change when you heard his name at the regatta.'

His mouth twisted. 'I overreacted. I know I did. It was just a shock finding out that you were working with him but I shouldn't have said what I did or fired you and I'm sorry.'

An apology. She stared up at him, mute and undone.

She shook her head, her eyes finding his. 'For him, not with him. He said he needed somebody "ethically flexible". A see-no-evil. Someone who would look the other way for the right price, and he knew all about my brothers, so I guess he thought I'd take the bait.' Her mouth trembled. 'And I did.'

'Because you love your family. That's a good thing, Sydney.'

'But I did a bad thing, and I'm sorry, and I know that doesn't change anything.'

'No, it doesn't.' He reached up and touched her cheek. 'But someone very smart and kind told me once that you can change how you think about the past.'

Their eyes locked and she held her breath, certain he would kiss her but instead he frowned.

'You're shivering.' Reaching past her, he grabbed the

throw and wrapped it around her shoulders. 'Come on, you need to get inside.'

Neither of them felt the need to speak on the walk back to the villa but as they walked into the bedroom, he stopped in front of her, his golden eyes fixing on her, so intent and direct that she hurt inside. 'What I said earlier about you being the hired help, I didn't mean it. Well, maybe I did in the moment, but that's not how I see you, and I don't want you to go.'

'I don't want to go either. Staying is the only way I'm going to get my brothers a good lawyer.' But that wasn't the only reason she didn't want to leave. She knew that. He did too. But she couldn't admit to it, because it was just too terrifying. Tiger clearly felt the same way, as he pretended to be taking it seriously, pulling out his phone.

'I can sort that out for you now.'

She shook her head. 'No, I know you're good for it.'

His gold eyes moved over her the way his hands had the other day in the half-light of the fisherman's hut. 'Oh, I am, am I? So if it's not my legal connections, what's making you stay?'

The air around them seemed to tremble. 'This,' she said softly. And she leaned forward and kissed him.

CHAPTER EIGHT

IT WASN'T A KISS, just a brush of her lips against his, but as she pulled away, Sydney could feel her body shaking inside.

'Do you—?' he began. 'Is this what you—?'

'Yes,' she said hoarsely.

If Tiger was fazed by the force of her words he gave no sign, he just closed the door and turned and reached for her in one movement, his mouth seeking hers, and she felt the heat radiating from him, and the hunger. The same hunger that was humming in her veins.

Only Tiger could quiet that chaos.

His hands were moving lightly over her body, caressing, pressing, stroking, his touch making her head spin, making her limbs tense with anticipation.

'Tell me what you want,' he whispered against her mouth. 'Tell me what you like.'

This, she thought, her heart pounding. She liked this. She liked the warmth of his breath and the way his thumbs were drawing circles on her belly. She liked him. Everything about him. But she didn't know what she wanted except that she wanted to see him unravel in the same way she had unravelled by the beach. And she wanted to take her time.

She pushed back from him, swaying a little, dazed by

that knowledge, by the certainty of her desire. 'I want it to be slow.'

The shutters weren't closed, and in the moonlight spilling through the window his golden eyes were molten heat. She saw him swallow, felt her belly clench, tightening hard with need as a muscle pulled at his jaw. And then his mouth was on hers and he kissed her as she had kissed him, softly, his lips barely grazing hers and then he pulled back to nip at her lower lip, taking his time, deepening the kiss a little more each time.

They kissed like that for some time. Just kissing, his hands flush against her hips, not moving, just steadying her and she felt her pulse slow, desire rippling through her in slow, curling waves.

She leaned into him and he lifted his hands so that she could take a step closer, close enough that she could feel the press of his erection against her stomach, hard where she was soft and yielding, and the feel of him made her shudder all the way through.

Yes.

His desire was the biggest turn-on and she arched her back, her hips meeting his, and, breaking the kiss, she tipped back her head, exposing her throat to his hot, teasing mouth.

A shivery pleasure danced across her skin and her hands moved to his chest as she moaned softly. He had a great body. Hard, muscular chest. Broad shoulders. And a stomach that made her fingers pluck his shirt from his waistband.

'Let me help,' he murmured and then he laughed softly

as she began tugging at his buttons. 'I thought you wanted to go slow.'

'I want to see you,' she said hoarsely.

His narrowed gaze was trained on her face. 'Then undress me.' His words sent shivers of need chasing across her skin.

Her pulse twitched, and she pulled his shirt down from his shoulders, then unbuttoned his trousers and hooked her fingers into the waistband and tugged them down his thighs, taking his underwear with them.

Oh, my—

He was naked now. And aroused. Very aroused.

Her skin was shivering as if she were cold, but flushed with the heat of her desire.

'My turn,' he said softly, and she tensed, her body hot and damp, and aching as he undid the buttons of her blouse and opened it to his gaze. Her lips parted as he slid his hand over the hot, bare skin of her stomach, and then tugged the blouse down over her shoulders.

Now he turned his attention to her skirt, deftly unfastening it.

She felt the air snap to attention as her skirt fluttered to the floor around her bare feet. She was naked now aside from her bra and panties and she felt his gaze like a caress, a whisper of heat and intent that made everything melt inside.

This was how she had wanted sex to be. Slow and seductive and thrillingly sensual.

He made her want so much. She could imagine his hands on her stomach and on her breasts and between her thighs.

There was a dark flush to his cheekbones and as she met his gaze, her belly tightened, then tightened again as he leaned in and fitted his mouth to hers, one hand cupping her cheek, his thumb brushing the skin there, his tongue, teasing her, stirring her senses. Making a kiss into something more than a kiss. Making it into a promise, a contract without words, that he was going to unravel her.

Heat flared inside her and she tried to deepen the kiss but he pulled back, tipped back her head to stare into her eyes.

'You're so beautiful,' he murmured, and, reaching up, he touched her mouth gently and she tensed for a different reason. But then he moved his thumb away and brushed his lips against hers, calming her.

'You're exquisite.' His hand slid down over her collarbone to cup her breast and her nipples tightened as he caressed first one then the other, lightly, before reaching round to expertly undo her bra. No one had ever touched her like this. No one had ever made her feel so hungry and uninhibited, so confident of her power to arouse, to take, to pleasure.

She sucked in a breath as he pushed her panties down over her thighs and stepped back, and she had to stop herself from crying out as the seconds ticked by and his gaze grew harder and hotter. And then he touched her lightly between the thighs and she moaned softly, her body instantly hot and tight and aching and damp for him.

Her hands fluttered down his torso to find his hands and then she lifted them up to cup her breasts. He sucked in a breath and now he lifted his mouth from her throat and she saw that he was fighting for control.

Yes, she thought.

She pushed him backwards, and he let her, bracing himself with his elbows as she dropped onto her knees. Her head was spinning. She had never wanted to do this with Noah. But the desire to taste Tiger, to give him pleasure in the same way that he had given her pleasure, was irresistible and, dipping her head, she flicked her tongue over the blunted tip, her hand wrapping around the length of him, and she took him in her mouth.

His hips jerked and he groaned, her clumsiness and lack of expertise no obstacle to his pleasure. Quite the contrary, she thought, his lack of control evident from the uncoordinated twitches of his body.

'Sydney.' He breathed out her name, his hand moving through her hair to still her, and she eased back and he pulled her onto the bed. Leaning back against the pillow, he put his hands on her hips and lifted her onto his lap and slid into her smoothly.

She moaned softly and he leaned forward, his mouth closing over her nipple, and she arched against him, shuddering, her hands gripping the muscles of his arm.

He pulled back then, his golden gaze dark and narrowed. 'Let me watch you,' he whispered and the hoarseness in his voice kicked up sparks inside her and she rolled her hips against his.

His face was taut with concentration, the muscles in his chest and arms bunching as his dark gold gaze held her and he began to rock his hips, one hand fitting into the indent at the base of her back, the other stroking her clitoris with his thumb.

She pressed against him, panting, chasing the flickering heat that was just out of reach and then he thrust upwards, driving into her and now she was trying to grip him, to hold him, to hold back but she couldn't.

Her body tensed, muscles tightening and tightening and tightening, in wave after wave, and he pulled her closer, burying his face against her throat as his body spasmed to a juddering climax.

A washed-out primrose light was seeping through the open shutters when Sydney blinked her eyes open. For a moment, she didn't recognise the room, then she felt the warmth of Tiger's body beside her and she remembered.

She remembered all of it.

Could see his body, so big and hard, moving inside her with shattering slowness. See herself, back arched like a bow, a creature of need and impulse, hardly human and yet all woman. The kind of woman she had always wanted to be. Powerful. Certain. Uninhibited and unafraid to be vulnerable.

It was different from the first time. Then their need for one another had been driven by frustration and a need to purge the jangling, seductive thing that had swirled around them.

Last night, this morning, was about desire and pleasure. Taking it and giving it. Because now she knew what desire looked like, what it felt like and tasted like. And she had wanted to feast on him, to lick every inch of his skin, to give him pleasure in the same way that he had pleasured her.

Now, though, it was time to leave. To give him space. And one less reason to regret what had happened?

Her limbs stiffened, her body protesting silently because she didn't want to leave the gravitational pull of his heat and his strength, and his gentleness. Remembering how lightly he had used his strength, she pressed her thighs together around the softness there and for a moment she let the feeling of being close to someone and not having to wonder if the hand clasping her waist would be tightening painfully around her wrist at any moment wash over her. She could enjoy the dizzying, unthinkable freedom of being in this space, with this man.

It was an astonishing sensation. But then it had been an astonishing, transformative night.

Tiger was a generous, intuitive, expert lover and being with him was revelatory. But it was more than knowing where and how to touch. Whatever was happening, however lost he was in his own ecstasy, she had sensed that a part of him was always tuned into her heartbeat and her breath almost as if they were joined by a thread.

Last night was about more than sex. They had fought and then they had talked. Tiger had talked about his father and his disastrous failed friendship with Harris Carver and she could see why he lived as he did, never letting anyone get close, choosing instead to walk by his 'wild lone'.

The people he had trusted had hurt him, betrayed his trust, made him feel vulnerable and powerless. No wonder he had decided that he wanted out. It was easier that way. And by easier he meant safer.

Suddenly it was hard to swallow past the lump in her throat. It was such a small ask. To feel safe. To be safe. Even for someone as rich and successful as Tiger, a life without safety meant a life not fully lived. A part of you was always curtailed by fear. Fear of failure. Fear of being hurt.

She hated that he had been hurt, was still hurting, and suddenly it was impossible not to reach out and touch his beautiful, sculpted face.

It seemed incredible to her now that back in New York she would have done anything to get out of being here with him. But it was going to end, and sooner rather than later. Much better to face that now while he slept. To draw a line now, rather than have it drawn for her as had happened so many times in the past. But also, because she was starting to care about him, and maybe she couldn't stop how she was feeling, but she didn't need to let it go any further.

Because last night had also been about reclaiming her power: the power to arouse; the power to act on her desire... and the power to leave.

Sliding out of Tiger's arms, Sydney shifted to the edge of the bed, moving carefully so that her progress wouldn't displace the mattress and disturb the sleeping man.

Get dressed, she told herself.

But that was harder to do than it sounded because her clothes were scattered haphazardly across the carpet like some confessional art installation.

'What are you doing?'

She froze.

Tiger was sitting up in bed, looking at her with sleepy eyes. Her gaze moved automatically to his gym-hard abs and then she remembered that she was naked. Which maybe explained why his eyes were looking a lot less sleepy.

'I thought you might want some space.'

'Don't you want to stay?'

She hesitated. He had told her the truth last night. But she was not brave like him, so this was as much of her truth as she was ever going to share. 'Yes, but I didn't know whether you would want that. I thought you might be regretting—'

'I'm not.' He shifted forward, his forehead creasing. 'Are you?'

His face didn't alter, but after last night she knew what it would have cost him to ask that, to admit a need of any kind, even just physical.

She shook her head. 'Not at all.'

The air in the room shifted, softening as if an unseen tension had lifted. 'So will you stay?'

He was watching her, waiting, she realised, for her to reply, to make her choice.

Her choice. The words fizzed on her tongue like sherbet. He was letting her choose, but he was also letting her know that he had no regrets. That he had wanted her and still wanted her, and knowing that made it easy for her to make her choice. To do what she wanted. To stay with him.

She nodded slowly and he moved then, kneeling up and holding out his hand.

'Come back to bed,' he said hoarsely. The sheet had fallen away from his body and, as if they were being pulled by some force of science or maybe nature, her eyes dropped to the erection standing starkly proud from his mouth-watering body. She felt her abdomen tense and an answering liquid heat between her thighs. He wanted her, and she wanted him. Why make it any more complicated than that?

Taking his hand, she let him pull her back to bed.

They spent most of the rest of the day in bed. Which was wonderful on so many levels, not least because it stopped Sydney panicking about the ball. The regatta had been fine, but it was more a 'day out' kind of atmosphere. There had been just so many people and so much noise that she had felt, not invisible, but lost in the crowd.

But the ball would be different. Instead of mingling with a drink in hand and smiling, there was a formal dinner, which meant having to make conversation. And then there was the dress. How was she supposed to carry off a ball gown?

'What are you worrying about?'

She jolted back to Tiger, nestling closer to his warm, solid body just for a moment before she answered. Just because she could. And because he was so gorgeous, and for the moment, anyway, he was hers.

'I was thinking about the ball, and the dinner.' Now she tilted her head back, met his eyes, felt another jolt at the curiosity there because he was listening to what she was saying. 'I've never been to anything like this. I mean, it's in a palace, for goodness' sake, and it's hosted by somebody called the Duke of Bergamo and Brandolini.'

Even just saying that out loud made her feel slightly sick.

Her breath caught as he pulled her towards him so that her breasts and stomach pressed against the honed muscles of his chest and abdomen.

'A ball is just a party. A palace is just a big house. And all those dukes and duchesses are just people like you and me.'

She rolled her eyes. 'But I'm not like you. You're like them. You own an island. And a private jet.'

'So, take them away. See what's left. That's when you realise that deep down people are all the same. Just think of it as a tailgate party with masks and champagne. And

I'll be there with you the whole time, so you don't need to be nervous.'

As he slid his hand along her cheek and smiled at her, she leant into it, groaning. 'You make it sound so easy.' She sounded casual enough, but her heart thudded inside her chest. With each passing minute, she found herself wanting him more. And she knew it was dangerous to think like that. To think that this was about anything more than sex. But that was hard to remember when he smiled like that.

Tiger waited for Sydney to join him downstairs, his fingers clamped around a slim, rectangular leather box.

His reaction to stress had always been to come out fighting, and his almost omnipresent state of anger with his father, and with the women who became his stepmothers, had left no room for nerves.

Until now.

He glanced up to the top of the staircase, and then swore softly as he realised what he'd done because he must have already looked up in anticipation of seeing Sydney there at least thirty times. And he didn't know why it mattered so much that she saw him looking up at her. He just knew that was what he wanted to do, and that waiting for her was making his stomach churn as if he were some gangly schoolboy on his first prom date.

Except he had been to plenty of proms and the girls had always been eager and ready. Was that why he was feeling so on edge? Because, inevitably, Sydney was making him wait and waiting was such an unfamiliar experience for him.

Maybe. But mostly he was nervous on her account.

He put the box down.

He had been telling her the truth when he said that the ball was just a party, but he knew that it would be intimidating and he wanted to give her this night. Wanted it to feel like a dream and for her to enjoy it and for her to shine, to recognise her own value.

His spine stiffened as he searched inside himself for the anger that had been a part of him for so long, but it was gone. Okay, he was angry with Harris for what he'd done. Mostly for what he'd done to Sydney, exploiting her like that. But it was a different kind of rage. It was clean, righteous, and, this was the biggest change, it was impermanent. Always before, his anger had been limitless and he'd never understood why. His whole life there had been no one to ask. His father, his stepmothers, his teachers, everyone had just seen the consequences, not the cause.

Only Sydney had bothered to ask. She had sat and listened and now he could see that his anger was just a form of weaponised fear. Fear of repeating his father's mistakes, of being used then abandoned. Of being part of someone's life and yet ultimately alone.

He didn't feel alone now. Or angry.

Here with Sydney, he felt relaxed, comfortable in his skin. Extremely comfortable in her skin too. Happy, basically—

His arms prickled and he saw something at the periphery of his vision and he turned, tilting his head back, and all the thoughts slid sideways, colliding with one another inside his head.

Sydney hadn't shown him which dress she was going

to wear, but given her nerves he'd assumed it would be something subtle.

She had gone bold. His eyes skimmed the rippling burnt-orange silk. No, it was more than bold. It was fearless, she was as fearless as a goddess, and just as beautiful.

'Don't talk to me,' she said, gripping the banister as she picked her way down the staircase. 'I have to concentrate otherwise I'm going to trip.'

As she reached the bottom of the stairs, he held out his hand, and she snatched it.

Their eyes met and, tilting her chin up, she smiled, and he smiled too because she knew she looked good and he liked that. But his opinion mattered to her. And he liked that too. He liked that a lot.

'You look good,' she said then.

And he was still so stunned that he just said, 'Thank you.'

Her face scrunched a little. 'I'm the one that should be thanking you.'

'For what?'

'For getting someone in to do my make-up and hair.' He glanced up to where her glorious red hair was coiled into some bouffant updo. 'And for this.' She smoothed a hand over the shimmering skirt. 'I've never worn anything so beautiful.'

His gaze moved over her face. He hadn't even noticed the make-up, but now, glancing down at her glossy lips, he wanted badly to kiss her.

'You look stunning.' His fingers tightened. 'I wanted to say that before… I was going to but…anyway, you look incredible, honestly, you look—'

'*Oh, sei bellissima, Signora—*'

It was Silvana, her hands fluttering to her cheeks, and he felt a rush of relief that she had arrived to stop him stammering like a schoolboy. And he hadn't felt this out of control since he was a kid. Had never wanted to feel out of control. That was why he lived as he did. Never committing, never allowing himself to care. Only he did care about Sydney. And that should be scaring him.

Then again, what was there to worry about? In a couple of days, they would go their separate ways, and his life would be back on track.

He cleared his throat. 'We should go.'

Sydney turned from where she was still being admired by Silvana and the maids.

'But first I have something for you for tonight.' He picked up the rectangular box he'd been clutching earlier. 'I didn't know what you were wearing so I went for diamonds because they go with everything.'

Her eyes were wide and stunned.

'Oh, Tiger, it's beautiful, thank you.'

'Here, let me put it on you.'

She turned and he picked up the necklace and looped it around her throat, fastening it at the nape.

It looked exquisite. The facets caught the shimmering fabric so that it looked as though there were flames flickering at the centre. The same flame he could see in her eyes and an answering heat flared inside him. Heat and hunger.

'Are you ready?'

The ball was the reason she was here. The reason he was here, but now he wished that he could just stay here with Sydney and talk and make love—

'Let's go,' he said lightly.

Tiger had wanted the evening to feel like a dream for Sydney. He hadn't expected it to feel like a dream for him too. Despite the glamour, he usually found these events boring and formulaic, but tonight, from the moment they had slipped on their masks and stepped off the *gondolino* and walked into the palazzo's glittering entrance hall, everything had felt as if it were in soft focus and weightless.

Only Sydney's hand in his felt real, and it seemed the most natural thing in the world to be with her. They sat opposite one another at the dinner, which meant he couldn't touch her, but he could watch her, and so while the spoilt heiresses on either side of him droned on, he watched Sydney. Watched and marvelled, because she was holding her own. More than that, she was shining.

After dinner, he got to hold her as they danced and every time her dress brushed against him, he would think about her body and how, even though she was turning heads in that dress, she looked better without clothes, and then he would try not to think about her naked because it made him want to stroke the soft skin of her thighs or trace his hand over the curve of her hip.

'Shall we go back?' he said, leaning in to graze his mouth against her throat.

Her eyes were bright and steady. 'Yes.'

As they walked off the dance floor, someone called his name, and he felt a hand on his shoulder and everything slammed into focus.

'McIntyre! I thought it was you.' Harry Atherton was grinning at him, swaying slightly, his eyes screwing up against the lights, his wife Juno clutching his arm. 'These bloody masks, honestly, if there's one thing I'd outlaw it would be masked balls.' He straightened slightly, his gaze sliding over Sydney. 'I'm sorry, we haven't been introduced.'

She smiled. 'Sydney.'

'Harry—it's a pleasure to meet you, Sydney. So, what are you two lovebirds up to now?'

Tiger felt Sydney glance up at him. 'I think we're going back to the villa.'

'Seriously, mate?' Harry frowned. 'We were all going to play some games upstairs. Come on, it will be fun.'

He tightened his hand into a fist. Maybe it was being recognised by Harry, but he felt suddenly disorientated and for a moment he was torn, but then again—

'Yeah, why not?'

'You know what we should do?' Juno shouted over the music. 'We should play hide and seek. Harry, you count and the rest of us will hide. Come on, Sydney.'

Juno dragged Sydney away and he stared after her, something jamming inside him as Harry started to count. It was just a game, and she was one of the few people on earth who had defied him, but that look on her face had been panic, fear almost.

He was moving before his brain caught up with his legs. Pushing past the other guests and up the stairs. Where was she?

'Hey, McIntyre, you're supposed to be hiding.'

He turned, eyes narrowing, and Harry stumbled back, holding his hands up. There was no reason to feel this panic, Tiger told himself, taking another flight of stairs, three steps at a time. But he couldn't seem to stop it. Yanking open a door, he stepped into the room.

It was small and unfurnished and empty, and he was about to leave when he heard it. The sound of someone breathing, small, panicky breaths almost as if they were injured. And then he saw her. She was pressed against the wall, her eyes closed, body shaking, one hand in front of her face as if she was trying to hide something.

'Sydney,' he said softly. 'Did someone hurt you?'

She was shaking her head, trying not to cry, he could see that now and it tore at him. He touched her wrist gently, wanting to comfort her, and her arm twitched and her eyes snapped open and then he saw her fear, and everything inside him turned to stone.

'It's okay. It's okay. I've got you,' he murmured, scooping her up into his arms. 'Just hold onto me. I'm going to take you home.'

CHAPTER NINE

LATER TIGER WOULD wonder how they got back to the island. He had a vague memory of walking downstairs, of shouldering his way through the crowds of partygoers, but beyond that nothing. Except Sydney's hand curled around his neck, limply, like a rescued animal.

He had felt a new kind of anger then. Not hot, but cold, cold enough to shatter everything it touched because he wanted to raze cities, wipe out populations, smash a world that could hurt a beautiful young woman and still keep spinning in space.

Remembering that blind flinch, he felt a dark heaviness spill through his chest. The pain he had felt as a child was nothing to this.

But his pain could wait. His anger too.

He slipped off his mask, then hers. 'Do you want me to get Silvana?' he said gently as Sydney sat down on the bed, staring past his shoulder, her freckles standing out against the paleness of her face.

She shook her head. 'I'm fine.'

Except she wasn't. Even if he hadn't heard the hollowness in her voice, he knew she wasn't fine. She looked exhausted and frozen to the bones, and she probably was in that dress. Getting up, he closed the shutters and then the curtains and then he crouched beside her. 'I think you should get into bed. I can help you undress or I can leave?'

She didn't answer, which he assumed meant that she wanted him to leave and he was about to stand up when her hand caught his. 'I don't want you to go.'

Her shoulder blades looked small and sharp like the wings of a moth as she leaned forward so that he could unbutton the back of her dress. He helped her into the T-shirt he assumed she wore in bed when she slept alone and then he undid her hair. And all the time he was helping her, he talked to her about nothing because he wanted to make it feel normal. Wanted to make her feel safe.

As she slid under the covers, he tucked her in. But she was still shivering.

'Let me get you something warm to drink.'

'Could you just stay for a bit?'

He nodded. 'I can stay. I can stay right here.' He stretched out beside her, still fully clothed, his head on the pillow beside her. 'Just close your eyes and try to get some rest. I'm not going anywhere.'

Her chest lifted and fell and then quite suddenly her eyes closed and she was asleep. He had planned on staying awake like some guard dog, but he must have fallen asleep too because he woke with a jolt and thought it was morning. But then he realised the lights were all still on and that Sydney's eyes were open, her face expressionless and watchful.

'Did I wake you?'

Shaking her head, she inched up against the pillows. 'I think I woke you.'

Her fingers were pleating the sheet and his heart felt as if it were going to slam through his ribs, but he had to ask. 'Did something happen there? Did someone hurt you?'

'No. No one did anything. It was my fault. I thought it would be okay. It's been so long, but—'

There was a silence and he could see her trying to marshal her thoughts and he wanted to pull her closer and hold her, but then he remembered how she had felt so limp and diminished when he'd carried her to the boat, and he knew that doing that would be for his benefit, not necessarily hers.

'You don't need to talk about it now. You don't need to talk about it ever.'

'I want to… It's been such a long time… I didn't think it would feel the same, because it was just a bit of fun. The hide and seek, I mean—'

'But it wasn't fun for you?' He knew it hadn't been, but he was terrified that she would shut down again if he pushed her.

She was shaking her head, shaking everywhere. 'I used to hide from him when he was really angry. Which was stupid, because I knew it would make him angrier, make him hurt me more.'

A wave of rage streaked through him like lightning. There was an excruciating pain in his chest, as if someone were snapping his ribs apart.

He looked at her still, tense body. Last night, she had helped him face the shame he had felt all his life. She had made him see his father in a different way and it had loosened the knotted ball of fear and distrust and anger so that it was easier to breathe. And all she had done was let him speak.

'Who hurt you, Sydney?' he said gently.

Her hands stilled against the sheet and for a moment she didn't respond. It looked as if she weren't breathing even, and he knew that she was reluctant to go back there. 'His name is Noah,' she said at last. 'Noah Barker and he was my husband.'

Husband. Tiger stared at her, his heart beating slow and hard in his chest, the air tilting around him. Sydney had been married? 'But not any more?'

The air in the room seemed to ripple as she shook her head. 'I left him five years ago, and then I divorced him.'

He could see then what he hadn't wanted to see in New York. What he hadn't been able to see because of his anger and confusion. Her defiance was an armour. That need to push back was self-defence learned the hard way.

'How long were you with him?'

'Just over a year. I should have left him after the first time. The first time he hit me. But he was so upset and he said it wouldn't happen again, that he would never let it happen again, and I believed him. Or maybe I wanted to believe him. I wanted what I thought he was offering.'

Tiger stared at her, light-headed with shock, his stomach lurching, the world exploding around him. He could hardly hold onto the thread of his thoughts.

'And he was my first. My only, until you.'

Her voice was scratchy and she seemed young then. He had a sudden, bruisingly clear memory of the two of them out in the hut by the beach. He remembered her hands pulling clumsily at his zip. He had put it down to the urgency of their hunger, but it had been her first time in five years.

'We were in this tiny flat and he thought we needed space, so we moved out to this house way out in the desert, and it was okay for a bit. And then it happened again and it kept happening. Only we were miles from anywhere and he had taken my phone and my credit card.'

She rubbed her forehead with her fingers as if it was hurting. 'I know what you're thinking. You think that I'm making excuses. That I should have left, that if I really wanted to, I would have left.'

Actually, he was thinking of all the ways he could ruin Noah Barker's life. Slowly, painfully.

He shook his head. 'Leaving is a process, not a single act. I sat next to the head of a women's refuge charity at some dinner. She told me it takes an average of seven attempts before a woman can leave.'

'It took me three.' She took a deep, shaky breath. 'The first time he dragged me back into the house by my hair. The second time I tried to take the car and he smashed my face into the steering wheel and knocked out a tooth. This one is an implant. The real one is in the desert somewhere.' Her voice trailed off and she pressed her fingers against her mouth as if she was remembering the pulpy feeling and the taste of blood.

'It kept bleeding so long Noah got worried and he took me to hospital. There was this nurse and she took me off on my own and she asked me if my husband had hurt me. I should have said yes, but I was so muddled and scared. After that I stopped running. I used to hide but that was worse. He used to get so angry.'

She made a small, tense gesture with her hand.

'Did your family know?'

He felt sick. The idea of hurting a woman was appalling but letting her be hurt was just as bad.

Her eyes skated away to the door. 'I didn't want them to know. I know it sounds crazy, but I was ashamed. I felt so stupid, and I thought it was my fault, that I was doing something to make him that way. That I deserved it.'

'Why would you ever think that?'

'Because for so long I hated being a Truitt. I love my family, but they don't make it easy. They're lazy and messy and they do dumb things.'

She sucked in a sharp breath. 'When I was growing up, we never had any money and they were always in and out of trouble, and I wanted to be different. I thought I was different, better than them, and I thought Noah was better because he dressed well and he had an expensive car, and an actual job, a good job. But he was a monster and it was my dumb, lazy brothers who rescued me.'

Her cheeks were shining with tears and Tiger reached into his pocket and handed her a handkerchief.

'The last time he hit me, he was so out of control. I remembered that nurse at the hospital and I stole his phone and I called Connor. I was so scared Noah would find out. He was always checking his phone and in the end I panicked and I dropped it into the oil tank.'

He hesitated a moment then put a hand on top of hers. 'And your brothers got there before he found out?'

Scrunching the handkerchief into a ball, she nodded.

'When Connor saw me, he wanted to kill Noah. They all did, but I wouldn't let them do anything, only then when I went to get my things Noah told me that I was a nothing. He spat in my face.'

Her face was wet again but there was a flicker of light in her eyes, a clear, unfaltering fire that he recognised.

'I punched him and I kept punching and Connor had to pull me off.'

He wanted to laugh, because of course Sydney had punched him, but instead he pulled her against him, kissing her face. 'Good for you,' he murmured, burying his face in her hair.

She looked up at him, smiling weakly.

'I didn't really hurt him but out of spite he must have called the police at some point and told them my brothers had assaulted him. They didn't tell me at first and then when I found out, they wouldn't let me go and tell them what really happened because they knew I didn't want anyone to know about Noah, and they didn't want me to get into trouble.'

'That's why you agreed to work for Harris,' he said slowly.

Her mouth was trembling, her hands too. 'I let them lie for me.'

Leaning back, he took hold of her wrists.

'Look at me, Sydney,' he said gently, but firmly. 'I don't know your brothers but I'm guessing they wanted to do that for you. And, yes, as a consequence they now have a criminal record for assault. But you didn't make them run a chop shop, did you? That's on them. And I won't let them go to prison. Whatever they need, I will make it happen, okay? You don't have to deal with this on your own any more, because you're not on your own. I'm here.' He softened his grip. 'Have you talked to anyone else about your marriage, like friends or counsellors?'

She hesitated, then shook her head.

'I went to a couple of DV support groups, but I didn't speak. I thought speaking about it would make it all come back and I just wanted to forget about it. You're the first, the only person I've told.'

Knowing that she had chosen him as her confidant made everything inside him spin like a pinwheel. 'If you need someone more qualified—'

'I don't think I do, but thank you. It's taken a long time but I can see now that Noah was the problem.' She swallowed. 'I think he knew his own limitations, and because of that he was angry at the world, and he took that anger out on me.'

'He did. He was a bully and a coward.' His gaze held hers, steady and direct. 'But just so we're clear, you did not deserve what he did to you. And you are not a nothing. You are brave and beautiful and loyal, and I am in awe of you.' He traced a line along the curve of her cheek. 'And, as you know, my opinion is the only opinion that counts.'

He pulled her back into his arms and held her tightly, and she tilted her face up to his and kissed him softly on the mouth. Then she pulled back and looked into his eyes and she kissed him again, this time with heat and longing.

'We don't have to.'

'I want to,' she said, finding his mouth again and pressing her lips to his. 'I want you.'

He rolled sideways, taking her with him so that she was on top.

'And I'm yours.'

* * *

Sydney stared down into Tiger's beautiful face, the air leaving her body. He meant here, now, in bed. And that was enough, she told herself. He was enough. In some ways, he was too much. Like his nickname, he changed the world as he moved through it.

Look what he had done for her.

Noah had broken her and she had put herself back together but nothing fitted, everything jarred and, because it hurt, she was reminded of the ugliness and the pain and fear. And it wasn't that she wanted to pretend that her marriage hadn't happened, but she couldn't move on.

But who couldn't face their fears with a tiger by their side? Thanks to him she felt whole and strongest along her fault lines. Whole and strong and freer than she'd ever felt before. It was as if she were filled with a golden light.

Her gaze moved shakily to his face, her pulse pounding in her head because it was him. Tiger. He had pushed back the shadows inside her, his strength and certainty, so different from the kind she had known before, pouring into her, hot and pure and clean like sunlight.

She felt dizzy. Her heart felt soft and vulnerable, no longer just an organ beating blood around her body but a rose, petals bursting apart, because that was what love felt like. And she had fallen in love with Tiger.

But how? When? The answer to all those questions was the same. Who cared? She was in love.

'Why are you smiling?'

She jolted back to him, glancing down at his gorgeous, golden face, feeling the press of his gorgeous, golden body, so gorgeous and male it made everything inside her feel sweet and honeyed.

Because I love you.

The words were there ready and waiting to spill from her lips, but how could she say them out loud?

They had known each other for such a short time that it could be counted in days. And he wasn't looking for love or even commitment.

'Because I'm happy.'

Small muscles creased around the corners of his eyes and he touched her face then, lightly, and, caught in his glittering gaze, she felt suddenly almost desperate to feel his mouth on hers, and his hands, and the hard length of him clenched between her legs.

Reaching down, she pulled her T-shirt up and over her head, feeling him still beneath her, and beneath the stillness a pulsing, predatory hunger that matched the hunger that was beating through her like a gong.

'I'm happy too now,' he said softly, and she laughed when she saw him smile, and she thought that if she could have one wish it would be that this moment would last for ever. Then he was reaching for her, stroking the swell of her breasts, and she was no longer capable of thinking.

They woke late again and took a long, warm shower together and then wandered downstairs. Smiling at two of the maids as they made their way out to the terrace, Sydney wondered if anyone could see the difference in her. It felt as if it should be visible because it felt like fireworks exploding beneath her skin. This was love, the thrilling, miraculous, absurd, mysterious, dreamlike, beautiful kind that was only supposed to happen in fairy tales.

And now that she knew what love really was, she knew that what she had felt for Noah was a pale, bloodless imitation of love, a delusion, a cruel trick. When she was eighteen, he'd seemed to represent all that glimmered only for the gilt to flake off and reveal dull lead beneath.

But Tiger, he was a ride on a roller coaster, all dips and tumbling turns and soaring upwards into a never-ending blue. He was also a safe haven, a lagoon in a stormy sea, and when his strong hands touched her skin, she could feel her scars healing. And his hands were touching her constantly. Even while they ate lunch out on the terrace, he kept reaching out to touch her almost as if she were necessary to him, like oxygen or daylight.

His phone buzzed and, pulling it from his pocket, he frowned.

'What is it?'

'It's the office. I'm sorry, but I'm going to have to deal with these emails.' He pressed her hand to his mouth and kissed it and she felt an intense, almost unbearable tug of hunger ripple through her body as she imagined leading him back upstairs to bed.

'Unfortunately, the business doesn't stop when I do.' He kissed her on the mouth then, and she tried not to read too much into his words. Tried to ignore the way it made her feel when he said things like that.

She'd thought he would disappear into his office, but he had lolled beside her on a lounger with his laptop and the fact that he had chosen to stay by her side simply added to the soft-focus happiness that seemed to burst from her skin every time they touched.

'I've been thinking about tomorrow,' he said slowly, sliding the laptop under the lounger.

The happiness oozed out of her. Tomorrow was always going to be her last day. On the flight over she had actually written those exact words in her diary and put a smiley face beside them. But now *my last day* sounded like an epitaph and she didn't feel like smiling any more.

'What are you thinking?' She lifted her hand to shield her eyes from the sun, but also to make it harder for him to see what she was thinking. His gaze seemed even more intense and golden than usual today.

'I've been planning a little surprise for Harris, retribution, you might say, for his meddling in our lives. But he will come out fighting, so I'd rather you weren't in New York when it goes live.'

'That's fine. I was going to go back to Los Angeles anyway.' Her throat tightened, but there was no reason to stay in New York. Or not one she could share with Tiger.

'You don't have to feel responsible for me.'

Her chest felt oddly tight. Or full, maybe that was a better description. But then she was breathing so much more easily today, maybe it was just all that extra oxygen.

'But I am,' he said slowly. 'So just stay in LA. Keep your head down. Maybe move back home for a while.'

'I can handle myself.'

'I know.' His eyes moved over her face. 'So how would you like to spend our last day?'

Sunlight was skimming across his face so that it was

hard to see his eyes but all too easy to imagine him stretched out above her.

'So what would you like to do? I want you to choose. We can do anything you want, go anywhere…just tell me what you like.'

'I know you've probably done it a hundred times already, but I'd really like to see Venice,' she said after a moment. 'Properly, I mean. You know, do the touristy things? Only, would that be too boring for you?'

Tiger stared down into her face.

Boredom was the secret curse of the super-rich. To a normal person a palace or a private jet was something you dreamed about. But to the top one per cent, they were assets, the adult equivalent of trading cards that you played with at school. With nothing out of reach, it was perilously easy to get bored.

But he couldn't imagine anything getting boring with Sydney.

It wasn't just the sex either. Right from the start, she had challenged him, challenged his status, and she was curious, which he loved. She wanted to learn, to explore, to lift up stones and see what was underneath. Character traits that made her such a good hacker. Such a good person.

'I can't think of anything I'd like to do better. Except go to the moon, but maybe we can do that next,' he said softly, and he felt his heart beat out a complicated rhythm as she smiled.

Making Sydney smile, making her happy, was not a burden but a pleasure, he thought as they made their way to St Mark's Square the following morning.

The hand that wasn't holding hers tightened into a fist. He couldn't understand how anyone could have hurt her, and with such systematic brutality. He hated to think of her alone and scared and trapped. Her ex deserved to be hung, drawn and quartered. And Sydney?

She deserved so much better. She deserved to be safe and happy, and more, so much more, and he couldn't give her everything she deserved but he could give her this.

He could give her Venice.

He gazed up at the Basilica with its great arches and Romanesque carvings and the four horses that presided over the whole piazza.

When he'd first made enough money to be able to leave the States and travel comfortably, he'd had a tick list of places to visit. All the usual suspects... London, Paris, Rome. But it was Venice that had fascinated him. There was a stubbornness to the city he liked, and an ingenuity that clicked with something in his brain. Then of course there was the architecture and the art and the food.

Since then, he had visited Venice as a 'tourist' on countless occasions, mostly on his own with a ball cap pulled down low over his face, his security detail discreetly matching his stride.

Visiting with Sydney was a whole lot more fun.

The landmarks felt less like scenes from postcards or backdrops to a thousand bloggers' selfies and she was wide-eyed with excitement, wanting to know everything. He had bought her a guidebook and he let her tell him the facts. The names of the buildings. The year they were built, and why. But then he told her the stories behind them.

'Casanova once escaped a tryst with the French ambassador and a couple of nuns by climbing across those rooftops,' he said, as they squinted up into the sunlight to admire the Doge's palace.

'And that house there,' he said, pointing to a long, low building on the Grand Canal. 'That's the Palazzo Venier dei Leoni. It was Peggy Guggenheim's home. She collected thousands of works of art during her time here, and thousands of lovers.'

Venice was not just a city, he thought as they sipped mimosas in Harry's Bar. It was a world of water, dappled and delicate, of reflections in tarnished mirrors, and each time he visited, he discovered something new. And Sydney was the same. With each corner they turned, he saw another, different side to her, each one more fascinating than the last.

And for once, he didn't try to navigate the confusion of side streets and sudden unexpected piazzas, because today the city itself seemed to be leading him somewhere.

They ate lunch in a *trattoria*. *Vongole* and red wine, watching the *vaporetti* glide past. And then, because he knew she wanted to, he suggested a ride in a *gondola*.

'Really?' She rolled her eyes. 'It's not too much of a cliché for you?'

He shrugged. 'I can't remember the last time I did this, so it feels new to me.'

No, that was her. He watched Sydney's face light up as he helped into the *gondola*. She made everything feel new and fresh and possible.

'Do you really want to go to the moon?' she asked him suddenly.

'Ever since I was a kid.'

'So the world isn't enough? You have to conquer space.'

Here, now with Sydney, it felt peerless but—

'Not conquer it. I supposed I just wanted to be some-place far away where I wouldn't have to deal with my dad's messes.'

She squeezed his hand.

'What do you think?' he asked as they glided down the Grand Canal, past the floating palaces with their filigreed, shuttered fronts.

'I think it's the loveliest place I've ever been.' Her ex-pression was so open and sweet it hurt to look at her. 'Maybe it's the water but there's something about the light here, it feels magical. I can't tell what's real and what isn't. I love it.'

'They say that other cities have admirers,' he said softly, responding to the happiness in her voice. 'But Venice has lovers.'

Their eyes locked. Lovers. The word hovered in the air between them and his blood began pounding fiercely through his body.

Was that what they were? Yes, but only in the physical sense, he told himself, because it was obvious that they were no longer just having sex. They were more than bod-ies fusing in mutual need. What they felt in each other's arms was more than pleasure. More complicated, but also less. There was understanding there and acceptance. Syd-ney had helped him face up to the pain of his past and ad-dress his anger with his father, and, frankly, that astonished him. She astonished him more and more with every pass-ing hour, and he cared about her.

But love—

Not being angry didn't mean he was ready or capable

of loving anyone. His childhood had left scars, and they would always be there and no matter how he and Sydney fitted together in bed and out of it. That wouldn't change.

He didn't want to admit that to himself, but Sydney needed, deserved, more than he could give. She deserved to be loved.

And he had a business to run and scores to settle. That was what mattered, that and not letting a week of intimacy and possibilities make him risk turning into his father.

She was staring at him, her hair loose around her face, brown eyes wide. She looked like a Titian and he had to kiss her then. Leaning forward, he pulled her closer and fitted his lips against hers gratefully, letting himself vanish in the kiss.

As they broke apart, he couldn't look away from the softness in her eyes.

'Shall we go back?' she said quietly.

Back at the island, they spent the rest of the day in bed, exploring, teasing, seducing one another. Finally, they lay, muscles relaxed, bodies warm and damp, their limbs intertwined, at ease with each other in a way that seemed both natural and miraculous. And yet something was different. He seemed distracted, as if his mind was split. Her heart squeezed a little. Could he be thinking what she was?

'Tiger.'

'Sydney.' His eyes gazed down on her, pupils darkening.

'Actually, hold that thought.' She leaned forward and kissed him on the mouth. 'I have to go to the bathroom.'

In the bathroom, she turned on the taps, scooping up the lukewarm water, to splash her face. Straightening, she stared at her reflection. Her heart was pounding. She hadn't needed the bathroom, but she'd had to leave. She needed some distance because it was getting harder and harder not to tell him that she loved him.

She wanted to, and she would, but she couldn't just hijack him with her feelings. He had been hurt, and just because she was ready didn't mean he would be. And that was fine. This was all still so new for her and she wanted to hold the feeling close and private. This feeling of love, of loving with knowledge and understanding, of loving a man who was worthy of her love, it made her feel strong and as if she were a bird soaring high and free.

For now, though, kissing him was easier.

'What was it you wanted to say?' he said, pulling her against him. She wriggled round so that her head was resting on his shoulder.

'I just wanted to thank you for taking me to Venice. It was the most perfect day.'

His eyes stilled on her face as if seeing her for the first time. 'It was. And thank you for being there for me this week. And I haven't forgotten about your brothers. I'll get in touch with my legal people on the flight home.'

Flight home.

She'd always known that they would be flying home this evening but hearing him say the words out loud was like having a bucket of cold water tipped over her head.

'So we're leaving this evening,' she said slowly.

He didn't speak or nod but he was already starting to sit up, shifting his weight. Retreating, she thought, her throat tightening.

'I have a meeting tomorrow with the lead on the space agency project. To talk numbers.'

He was standing now, and had already pulled on his trousers. 'And maybe finalise my piggybacking on one of the exploratory missions.'

'So you really are going to go to the moon? That's amazing. I'm so pleased for you.' Her smile was instant and genuine. His face softened a fraction and he pulled her closer, his hand curving around her waist.

'Hopefully, yes.'

He let go of her then without even kissing her and she stared at him in confusion.

'Don't look so worried. You kept your side of the deal and I'm going to keep mine. I'll make sure your brothers get the best legal counsel.'

The deal. She stared at him, trying to breathe past the frozen lump in her chest. He must be trying to reassure her because there was more to this week than the deal they'd made in New York.

'I just thought—'

'Thought what?' he said impatiently. 'Look, Sydney, I know things have got a little blurred between us but this was only ever a temporary arrangement. '

Her heart stumbled. He was looking at her in the same way as he had a moment earlier and she felt a chill scamper down her spine because she wasn't the stranger here. He was. There was a tension in him now, and a distance.

She cleared her throat. 'Maybe I could come with you,' she said lightly. 'You know, watch your back. Support you.'

He ran his hand through his hair. 'Where is this coming

from, Sydney? I don't need supporting. What I need is for you to stick to the terms of our arrangement.'

Glancing down, she realised she was naked and she reached for her robe. As she slipped it on, something flickered in his eyes, desire, and something else she couldn't name.

'I don't care about the terms of our arrangement. I care about you. And I thought you cared about me. You said you did.'

Tiger was staring at her, his eyes not that clear, light gold any more, but opaque, guarded.

'I did say that, and I meant it. In the context of you being here. With me. Now.'

The room seemed to sway a little. Here. Now. The terms of the deal had been clear from the start. Nothing had changed, and everything had. She watched him shrug on his jacket to complete his transformation back into the billionaire tycoon she had met in New York.

He glanced over at her, his forehead creasing. 'I can make sure you're taken care of. I can make things happen for you. Good things. You have excellent skills so maybe so if you still want that job at McIntyre—'

'You're offering me a job?' She felt dazed, drunk almost. 'I don't want to work for you, Tiger.'

'That's fine. If you'd prefer to work for another company, I can make a few calls, put in a good word for you.'

She was shaking her head. Her whole body was shaking. 'I don't want to work for you and I don't want you to put in a good word for me. I love you.'

She had said it before but not understood what it meant. Now she did, and she felt it spinning inside her like sugar turning to candyfloss. 'I love you,' she said again. Because he was worth the risk. They were worth the risk.

But Tiger was staring at her as if she had said a different kind of four-letter word. A shadow slid across the curve of his cheekbone. 'I'm sorry, Sydney. I think you are an incredible woman—'

'Don't do this, don't pretend—'

'But this is pretend,' he said flatly. 'It's only ever been a pretence, a performance.'

'I don't believe you.' Her chest felt tight, and heavy. 'I know you. I know this is real.' It was difficult to breathe, to speak, but she had to try. 'You're not your father, Tiger.'

'Maybe not, but I can't be what you need, what you deserve.' His eyes were dull like beaten metal. 'I'll call my lawyers *en route*.'

'No, I'll find another way.'

His gold eyes were darker than a solar eclipse. 'Do me a favour. Maybe stay here until the stuff with Harris blows over.'

He stared at her for a moment and then he turned and walked swiftly through the door. Outside, she could hear the waves splashing against the shore. The world was still shifting, moving, breathing. But as she slid to the floor, hugging her knees to her chest, she knew she would never be a part of it again.

CHAPTER TEN

SYDNEY HADN'T STAYED on the island.

Tiger shifted back in his chair and stared across his office, remembering that first time he'd seen her out of the corner of his eye, all light curves and red hair.

Because that was the problem: there was too much to forget and so much he wanted to remember.

About an hour after take-off, he'd swallowed his pride and made a call to Silvana. Even though he'd still been piqued by her outburst as he was leaving. It was the first, the only time, he could remember his housekeeper losing her temper with him, and in English.

'Why are you leaving?'

'Because I have a business to run,' he'd countered.

Silvana had folded her arms across her body and stared at him. 'And what about Ms Truitt?'

He'd frowned. 'What about her?'

Her eyes had narrowed. 'Why is she not with you?'

'She's not with me. She never was. This was only ever a short-term thing.'

Silvana had snorted. 'Short term? I saw how you looked at her when she came downstairs before the ball. That is not how a man looks at a woman who is short term to him.'

He had been rooted to the spot. With fury and fear. Because he could still remember how he had felt. *Felt.* So many feelings roaring through him, and he hadn't recognised half of them, and hadn't known what to do with any of them. Or what it meant that he felt them for Sydney.

'I know you are scared of loving.' Silvana's face had softened. 'And it is scary because loving hurts but losing her will hurt worse. So don't leave her here. Stay or take her with you. That is what you want. She wants it too.'

'I can't do that.'

'Then you are a fool.'

No fool like an old fool. It was what people said about his father. That Silvana could say it to him made him see red, and he had stormed off without another word.

On the phone, he had made up some nonsense about papers on his desk. But really it had been an excuse to check that Sydney was okay.

His hands had tightened against the armrests.

'Lei non è qui, Signor McIntyre,' Silvana had said tersely. *'Se n'è andata circa due ore fa.'*

In other words, Sydney had left right after him.

Pushing away from the chair, he strode over to the windows, his pulse beating out of time. He had tried to call her, but her number was out of service and her website just offered a message of apology. In other words, she had gone dark.

He felt a flicker of frustration, and beneath that a nagging anxiety that Sydney was out there in the world without him. Not that he was worried about Harris. When the story finally went live, he would be too busy salvaging his reputation to go after Sydney.

But he couldn't stop thinking about how he'd ended things. Or the look on her face. He had told himself countless times that it had to be that way. That she knew what she was signing up to. All the things he'd told himself in the past, and it had never been a problem before.

Only it was now. For some reason he couldn't explain, he couldn't unhear her telling him she loved him. Couldn't unsee the moment when he'd told her it was a pretence. The look on her face as she'd looked up at him had sliced him open.

Because he cared about Sydney. How could he not after everything she had told him? But this feeling he had, this tightness in his chest that made it hard to catch his breath, and the waking in the night and the inability to focus on anything, it was probably just a virus, something he'd picked up crossing six time zones.

He gazed out across New York, a memory stirring inside him like a flickering flame: of him taking Sydney's arm and leading her to the window to show her the view. It cost a lot of money to own that view. As he looked at it now, it held no value.

Nothing seemed to have any value any more, not even the contract that would take his empire into space.

Because Sydney wasn't here with him.

He let his head fall against the glass, trying to cool his feverish brain, but it wasn't a fever making him feel like this. It wasn't down to something he'd picked up. It was something he'd lost. No, pushed away.

His eyes were burning. The irony was that he had spent his whole life not wanting to be like his father. Not wanting

to be tricked by 'love' because he had seen only the false-
ness of love and how it diminished everything it touched.

But Sydney did love him. He knew that because he knew
her. He had fought with her and comforted her and held her
while they made love and she had held and comforted him.
They had talked and listened and laughed and she had cried.

She loved him. It wasn't a pretence.

And that was why he couldn't be with her. Because he
loved her too. He pressed his hands against the glass, fram-
ing that truth, accepting it, acknowledging it. Letting it
push back all the layers of fear and the assumptions he'd
made and clung to for so many years.

He had loved her from that very first day in his office.
He just hadn't seen it because he hadn't known what it was.
Not even at the masked ball when he had been so hope-
lessly in love with her that his housekeeper and the maids
had known. Give a man a mask, and he will tell the truth.
He had told the truth that night, but had been too blinded
by fear of falling into the same bad pattern of behaviour
as his father.

He saw it now. He felt it now, inside him, burning bright
and pure like a votive flame.

Only he was so untested in love, so unpractised, and he
wanted the best for her. Wanted to protect her. That was
why he'd wanted her to stay on the island. That was what
he'd told himself. Maybe, though, keeping her on the island was more about prolonging the fantasy, because the
reality of love still scared him. Silvana knew that, Sydney
too. But it had taken losing her for him to see it, and his
housekeeper was right, losing her hurt more. And it was a
self-inflicted pain. By attempting to avoid the pain of love,

he had pushed Sydney away and hurt himself. Hurt her too, just as his father had hurt him. Because it was people who hurt each other and sometimes they used love as an excuse.

And he needed to tell her that he'd been wrong, and stupid. A fool, in fact.

Breathing out unsteadily, he lifted his head.

Was it too late?

No, it couldn't be, was the only answer to that question that he could contemplate. But if he was going to be the man Sydney needed by her side, then, for the first time in his life, he was going to have to take a leaf out of his father's book and take a risk on love.

'It should only take a couple of hours but if you need us, all you have to do is call.'

'Why would I need you?'

Glancing up from the magazine she had been pretending to read, Sydney frowned at her brother. She had been helping out at the auto repair shop for the last few days, partly to have something to take her mind off Tiger and partly because she wanted the judge to know that this was a genuine family business.

'It's lunchtime. Nobody has come in at lunchtime for the last three days.'

Connor reached past her to grab the keys to the pick-up. 'Yeah, but if they did and you didn't know something, you can call us is what I'm saying.'

Her middle brother, Jimmy, nodded. 'We're only talking to her. It's not like we're in court.'

'She's your lawyer. You need to pay attention to what she's saying. Don't take any calls. In fact, switch off your phones.' She put down the magazine, frowning. 'Maybe I should come too.'

This was the penultimate meeting with the lawyer before they went to the courthouse on Tuesday. Kim Shaw had been a good pick. She was smart, no-nonsense but she had also agreed to being paid in instalments. Which was surprising but also a great relief. Sydney hadn't asked Tiger to make good on his promise. She had thought about it. Not seeing him in person—just thinking about that had made her want to curl into a ball and howl. But she had considered calling him—and almost immediately decided against it.

What they'd shared might never have been real to Tiger, but she had loved him, utterly and unconditionally and, despite how it had ended, she didn't regret it. But asking him to get a lawyer for her brothers would take that love and turn it into something ugly and transactional.

'It's fine. We're just signing some paperwork. We're seeing her again on Monday to go through everything.' Her youngest brother, Tate, leaned in and kissed her on the cheek. 'Besides, we need you here otherwise we'll have to shut up shop.'

'Don't forget to switch off your phones,' she called after them. 'And stop looking so shifty.' They were looking shifty, she thought as she watched them leave, her heart thudding against her ribs. But she loved them all the same, and it looked as if they were going to avoid jail time, so having her heart broken by a beautiful stranger had been worth it.

Except Tiger wasn't a stranger to her. Leaving Italy, she had felt bereft, as if she had left her shadow behind.

The journey back to the States was a blur, but somehow

she had got to Los Angeles and gone like a homing pigeon to her parents' house.

This was the second time she had moved back home after her life had imploded. The difference was that then the hurt had had relief in it. Now, though, she felt alone and desperately, desperately sad.

She missed Tiger. All the time that she was awake, she missed him constantly and so intensely that sometimes she would have to press her hand against her chest to push back against the ache there. And at night, she dreamed about him. Hot, frantic dreams where he felt so real that she would wake with a start, expecting to hear his voice, talking to her in that same soft, soothing way that he had after the ball. His arms holding her tightly, his heart beating through her and steadying her.

But it was just her, alone, in the bed she had slept in as a child. And it was there in that bed, alone in the darkness, that she allowed herself to cry.

She hadn't told her family anything of what had happened with Tiger. She just didn't have the words. How could she describe that astonishing, life-changing *coup de foudre* of meeting a man like him and of finding herself in his golden gaze?

How could she describe the intensity of their dizzying chemistry? Or the rightness of his body against hers? It would sound ridiculous when in fact it was miraculous, transformative, a benediction, an awakening.

Thinking about him hurt so much. Loving him was like having a splinter of ice in her heart. But then she should have known. Tiger's heart was off-limits. Hopefully, one day, someone would find the key to set him free and let him love as she knew he could and should love. With fire and fervour.

As for her, she had to rebuild her life. Try to live an hour, then a day, then a week and so on.

And she would do it.

Right now, she had shut down Orb Weaver, but it was only temporary. She needed to focus on keeping her brothers out of prison. And as soon as she knew they were safe and free, she was going to go travelling to Europe. To London and Paris and Copenhagen and Barcelona, and then maybe she could think about going back to Italy.

After that? Who knew? Maybe run the business out of some London town house? Or perhaps she would just come back to LA. Right now, she was taking one day at a time.

Speaking of which, she needed to change the battery in the clock. The time had been stuck at half past ten for about three years now.

But where did Connor keep the batteries? She found them in the end, and she took the clock down off the wall and began pushing them into the slot. No, that was wrong. She had put the positives and the negatives back to front.

The door buzzer made her jump, but she didn't look up. At this time of day, it was probably just the guy from office supplies. She was trying to make the auto repair shop look more professional and less like a hang-out for wannabe gangsters.

'Be right with you.'

'In your own time.'

That voice. The air around her froze. Her whole body stilled, even her heart stopped beating. For days now, it had been as if she were wearing an old-fashioned diver's suit, the kind with the fishbowl helmet, and she'd had to focus hard to work out what the people on the other side of the glass were saying. But his voice had cut through the glass instantly.

She felt a jolt against her ribs as her heart started again and the roar of her own blood spun her round to face him.

No name needed, because 'him' could mean only one man.

Tiger was standing in the doorway, his fingers loose around the handle. And the world snapped into focus, so real and sharp it hurt, his beauty blinding her like a search-light. She stared at him in shock, stunned, devastated.

She must be imagining him. Except she wasn't.

'We're closed.'

He shut the door, and flipped the sign. 'Yes, you are.'

Still arrogant, she thought, arrogant and wanting to run things his way.

For an endless, shuddering moment, nothing happened and then he walked slowly towards her with that beautiful feline grace as if he owned this shabby little shop. As if he owned the whole world. But he didn't own her.

She slammed her way round the desk. 'You need to leave.'

'We need to talk.'

'No, we don't,' she snapped, trying to manage the vault-ing somersaults her heart was performing beneath her ribs at the same time as stifling the shoot of hope she could feel trying to push its way to the surface. Because seeing him was already too much for her to handle.

'Your phone number doesn't work. Your website is inactive. And you closed your bank account.' His voice was quiet but she could hear his anger and frustration.

'I already know all of that.' Her voice cracked and she stared at him, shaking, not with fear, but with need and longing, and love. But Tiger didn't love her.

Tilting her chin, she forced herself to look into his eyes. 'So, if that's all you came to tell me, I think we're done here.' She didn't want to believe it, but now that she had said it out loud, she meant it.

'Why did you do that? I was going to help you. You need the money.'

She folded her arms in front of her aching chest. 'Not your money. And what I do with my bank account is none of your business.'

Tiger felt his heartbeat accelerate.

Walking into the auto repair shop and seeing Sydney there, whole, not weeping or bleeding or crushed, he had felt a bone-deep relief and such an immensity of love that he could hardly speak. Because he knew what love was now. He knew because it no longer felt like a risk but an adventure, a poem and a blessing all rolled into one.

But it was as if she were still behind the glass counter. There was a barrier between them, thin but unwavering, which was good. He wanted her to be safe and careful. But also bad, because he wanted to take her in his arms more than he had wanted anything, even the moon.

Only he needed to find the right words.

'It is my business. You are my business.' Which were the wrong words, he realised, cursing silently, panic swelling in his throat as he watched her stiffen. He tried again. 'What I'm trying to say is that you're my world.'

'And you're heading to the moon, so you'll be orbiting me at a distance, which suits me fine.'

'Not without you. If I go, you go.'

'You can't do this, Tiger. You can't just turn up and say things like that. I was getting better. So say whatever it is you came here to say, and then go.'

His heart felt as if it were tearing in two. All his life he had seen love as a weakness but now that it filled him from head to toe, it felt like a superpower. Only one that he hadn't learned how to use properly.

Please let me find the words, he prayed.

'It's very simple really. I love you and I need you. And I don't know how to live my life without you. Without you, nothing matters. Nothing makes sense.'

'You're the one not making sense. You told me you didn't love me. You chose the moon, remember?'

'I don't care about the moon. I care about you. And I love you. I love you like I never thought it would be possible to love anyone. And I know you probably won't believe me, but I think I loved you right from when you walked into my office and gave me the cold shoulder. I just didn't know what I was feeling. But I was lucky. I had a couple of people on hand to help me and I took their advice.'

Her eyes, her beautiful brown eyes, were wide and stunned. 'Your lawyers told you to come and find me?'

He shook his head, then he took a step forward. Just a small one, not big enough to scare her.

'When I was leaving the island, Silvana gave me a ticking-off. Made me see that I was sabotaging the only future that's ever made sense to me. The only future I want, and need.'

She held his gaze. 'What did she say?'

He laughed. 'She told me a few home truths.' Another step forward. 'Basically, that I was a fool.'

'You're not a fool.'

His eyes on hers were bright with tears, and as he shook his head, she took a step this time. 'I walked away. I let you slip through my fingers.' He hesitated, then reached out and touched her cheek gently, his heart contracting with relief, and a hope that hurt, when she didn't pull away. 'That would make me a fool in anyone's book.'

'Never to me.' She let herself lean close because he was so familiar, so beautiful and she couldn't not. 'You said a couple of people. Who was the second?'

'My father.' His mouth twisted. 'I remembered you saying that he thought it was worth risking everything for love. And I realised that I was risking everything that mattered to me because I was *scared of* loving you, of losing you. And then I lost you anyway.'

'You haven't lost me.'

Tears filled her eyes as he made a hard, scratchy noise as if his throat were too tight. 'I know that I have no right to ask for a second chance but, back in Italy, you said you loved me and I was hoping you might still feel that way.'

'You know I do,' she said softly, and he pulled her against him now, grateful that he had been given this second chance.

'And I love you. You believe me, don't you?'

Sydney looked up at him, seeing a man with a beautiful face and a loving heart. Strong still, but with the hard edges rubbed off. He had shone a light into her darkness and she loved him utterly, and unconditionally. 'I know you're good for it.'

He laughed again, and they moved closer, then apart, then closer again, like waves tumbling onto the shoreline, amazed by each other, stunned by the miracle of it.

'When did you get here?'

'Yesterday. I've been going out of my mind waiting. But I knew you'd need persuading, so I had to wait until you were on your own.'

'But how did you know I was going to be on my own?' She frowned, remembering Connor's shifty expression. In fact, they had all looked shifty. 'Did my brothers know you were coming here? They did, didn't they? I knew they were being weird.'

'Not weird. Worried. They care about you. A lot.' Remembering the triple-tractor-beam intensity of their gaze, he smiled at her. 'They needed persuading too, believe me. I think one of them mentioned a shotgun and a shovel at one point. But I explained why I needed to talk to you, and I asked for their help.'

'I can't believe you talked to my brothers.'

'Of course, I did.'

'Why of course?'

He shrugged. 'If we're going to be related, I need to get to know them, don't you think?'

Related?

She stared at him mutely. Her head was spinning. She felt as though she were floating. 'I don't understand. What do you mean by "related"?' Her voice trailed off and she covered her mouth with her hand. Tiger was kneeling down on the dusty floor, holding out a diamond ring.

'Marry me, Sydney,' he said softly.

Her legs folded beneath her and she slid down beside him. 'You can't do this. We can't do this,' she said hoarsely.

'Is that a yes?' he managed.

'Of course it's a yes.' Her hands tightened on his arms and for a moment he couldn't breathe past her words. 'But you're here and I don't want to lose you again.'

'You can't lose me. When I got on that plane to fly back to New York, I was fighting you, fighting myself, fighting Silvana because everything I thought was true and necessary for me was slipping away or disintegrating and that scared me because there was nothing left to hold onto. But then I realised that the only thing I wanted to hold was you.'

'But we've only known each other for a few days.'

'Ten.' He smiled at her, and just like that she was lost or maybe found. 'But who's counting?'

'Everyone will. They'll say we don't know each other. They'll say that we need more time.'

'We do know each other, and we're going to have for ever.' He pulled her close, his heart beating like a drum, pressing her close to him, breathing in her scent and her strength.

'And as you already know, although it seems I might have to remind you again, the only opinion that matters on that subject is mine. And it's not just an opinion.' He lifted his chin and there was a dark gleam in his eyes that made her breath catch. 'It's more of a directive.'

'Is that right?'

'It is,' he said softly, and, dipping his head, he found her mouth with his and set about proving that to her.

* * * * *